The Italian Girl

THE
Italian Girl

A NOVEL BY
Iris Murdoch

New York · The Viking Press

Published in 1964 by The Viking Press, Inc.
625 Madison Avenue, New York, N.Y. 10022

Library of Congress catalog card number: 64-18481
Printed in U.S.A. by The Colonial Press Inc.

To Patsy and John Grigg

Contents

TWO

THREE

ONE

1 🌹 *A Moonlight Engraving*

I pressed the door gently. It had always been left open at night in the old days. When I became quite certain that it was locked I stepped back into the moonlight and looked up at the house. Although it was barely midnight there was not a light showing. They were all abed and asleep. I felt a resentment against them. I had expected a vigil, for her, and for me.

I moved through a soft tide of groundsel and small thistles to try the two front casements, but they were both firm and a greater blackness breathed at me from within. Calling out or throwing stones at windows in such a silence, these were abhorrent things. Yet to wait quietly in the light of the moon, a solitary excluded man, an intruder, this was abhorrent too. I walked a little, with dewy steps, and my shadow, thin and darkest blue, detached itself from the bulk of the house and stealthily followed. At the side it was all dark too and protected by such a dense jungle of ash saplings and young elder trees that it would have been impossible to reach a window, even had there been one unlatched. I measured, by the growth of these rank neglected plants, how long it was since I had last been in the north: it must be all of six years.

It had been foolish, entirely foolish, to come. I ought to have come earlier when she was ill, earlier when she wanted me and wrote in letters which for anger and guilt I could scarcely bear to read, come, come, come. To have come then would have made sense in the light of the last abstract consideration I had for her: after all she was my mother. But to come now that she was dead, to come merely to bury her, to stand in her dead presence with those half-strangers my brother and my sister-in-law, this was senseless, a mere self-punishment.

I returned across the lawn, following my own tracks in the dew. The clouded moon had spread a luminous transparent limb across the sky and showed me the silhouettes of the great trees which surrounded the house. It was still the skyline I knew best in the world. I felt for a moment almost tempted to go away, to try the door once again and then to go, like the mysterious traveller of the poem. "Tell them I came and no one answered." I looked again at the familiar shapes of the trees and shivered at the sudden proximity of my childhood. There were the old June smells, the wet-midsummer-night smells, the sound of the river and the distant waterfall. An owl hooted, slowly, deliberately, casting out, one inside the other, his expanding rings of sound. That too I remembered.

The thought that I might go away and leave them all there asleep made me pause with a sort of elation. There was an air of vengeance about it. That would be to leave them forever, since, if I went away now, I was sure I would never return. Indeed, whatever happened, I would probably never, after this one time, return. My mother's existence here had been the reason for my not coming. Now her non-existence would provide an even stronger reason.

I must have been standing there for some time in a sad reverie when I saw what for a weird second looked like a reflection of myself. I had so vividly, I now realized, pictured myself as a dark figure upon that silver expanse that when I saw, emerged into the dim light in front of me, another such figure, I thought it could only be me. I shivered, first with this weird intuition, and the next moment with a more ordinary nervousness of this second night intruder. I knew at once from the outline of the man that it was not my brother Otto. Otto and I are both very big men, but

Otto is bigger, although his stooping six-foot-three may pass for no more than my upright six-foot-one. The figure that now slowly advanced towards me was small and slim.

Although I am not especially a coward, I have always been afraid of the dark and of things that happen in the dark: and this night illumination was worse than darkness. The sense that I was also frightening the other man simply made me more alarmed. In a horrible silence I moved slowly towards him until we were near enough to catch a glint from each other's eyes.

A soft voice said, "Ah—you must be the brother."

"Yes. Who are you?"

"I am your brother's apprentice. My name is David Levkin. For a moment you frightened me. Are you locked out?"

"Yes." I hated saying this to him, and suddenly all my old love for the place, my old patriotism for it, filled me with pain. I was locked out. It was monstrous.

"Don't worry. I'll let you in. They are all gone to bed."

He moved across the lawn to the shadow of the house and I followed him. The moonlight fell in streaks through the overgrown lattice of the porch weighed down with honeysuckle, and revealed the fumbling hand and the key. Then the door gave softly to show the thick waiting blackness of the house, and I followed the boy out of the honeysuckle fragrance into the old stuffy, foxy darkness of the hall. The door closed and he turned on a light and we looked at each other.

I recalled now that my sister-in-law Isabel, the news-giver of the family, had written to me some time ago about a new apprentice. Otto's apprentices were something of a sad tale and a cause of scandal always to my mother. With unerring care he had attracted to himself a notable sequence of juvenile delinquents, each one worse than the last. I scanned the boy but could not for the moment recall anything Isabel had said about him. He seemed about twenty. He did not look English. He was slim and long-necked, with big prominent lips and a lot of very straight brown hair. His nose was wide, with big suspicious nostrils, and he eyed me now with narrow eyes, very doubtfully, his lips apart. Then he smiled, and as the eyes almost vanished the cheeks broadened out in great wreaths of welcome. "So you have come."

The locution might have been impertinent or merely foreign. I could not see his face properly. My mother, intensely mean with money, had always insisted on using the weakest possible electric-light bulbs, so that there was scarcely more to be seen within than by the light of the moon. It was a weak, dirty, weary sort of dimness. I wished to be rid of him and said, "Thank you. I can look after myself now."

"I do not sleep in the house." He said it solemnly and now with a perceptible foreignness. "You will know where to go?"

"Yes, thank you. I can always wake my brother."

"He does not sleep in the house now either."

I felt unable to discuss this. I felt suddenly utterly tired and ill-used. "Well, good night, and thank you for letting me in."

"Good night." He was gone, dissolving in the pale, uncertain yellow light, and the door was closing. I turned and began to go slowly up the stairs with my suitcase.

At the top of the stairs I paused as the familiar pattern of the house seemed to enter into my body magnetically: Otto's room, my room, my father's room, my mother's room. I turned towards my own room, where I assumed a bed would have been made up for me; and then I paused. I had not yet really conceived of her as dead. I had thought about journeys and times, about the cremation which was to take place tomorrow, about the nature of the ceremony, about Otto, even about the property, but not about her. My thoughts, my feelings about her belonged to some other dimension of time, belonged to before whatever it was that had happened to her twenty-four or thirty-six hours ago. The sense of her mortality invaded me now, and it became inevitable that I should enter her room.

The dim electric light revealed the big landing, the oak chest and the fern which never grew but never died either, the fine but entirely threadbare Shiraz rug, the picture which might have been by Constable but wasn't, which my father had got in a sale, at a price for which my mother never forgave him: and the closed, silent doors of the rooms. Before the sick feeling should make me feel positively faint I went to my mother's door and quickly opened it and turned on the light within.

I had not expected her face to be uncovered. I closed the door behind me and leaned back against it with a violently beating heart. She lay, raised up rather high upon the pillows, her eyes closed and her hair undone. She could not have been sleeping, though it would have been hard to say quite how this was evident. Her face was a yellowish white and narrowed, shrunk already away from life, altogether smaller. But her long hair, which had been bronze once, now a dark brown striped with grey, seemed vital still, as if the terrible news had not yet come to it. It seemed even to move a little at my entrance, perhaps in a slight draught from the door. Her dead face had an expression which I had known upon it in life, a sort of soft crazed expression, like a Grünewald Saint Anthony, a look of elated madness and suffering.

My mother's name was Lydia, and she had always insisted that we call her by this name. This had displeased my father, but he did not cross her in this or indeed in anything else. My mother's affections had early turned away from her husband and focused with rapacious violence upon her sons, with whom she had had, as it were, a series of love affairs, transferring the

centre of her affection to and fro between us, so that
our childhood passed in an alternate frenzy of jealousy
and of suffocation. In my first memories she was in
love with Otto, who is my senior by two years. When
I was six she loved me passionately, and again when I
was ten, and again in my later years at school; and
perhaps later too, and most fiercely of all, when she
felt me slipping from her grasp. It was when it was at
last clear to her that I had escaped, that I had run away
and would not come back, that she turned her emotions onto her last love, her granddaughter, Flora, Otto
and Isabel's only child. She would often say that no
one but she could control the little girl. It was true:
Lydia had seen to it that it was true.

She was a small woman. She had been so proud,
when we were at art school, of her two huge talented
sons. I can recall her walking between us and looking
up at each in turn with a proud possessive leer, while
we stared ahead and affected not to notice. She was, in
some way, a great spirit; all that power, with some turn
of the screw, might have organized some notable em-
pire. There was nothing of the artist in her. Yet with
this she was a timid woman, convinced of the hostility
of the world and incapable of crossing a hotel lounge
without believing that everyone there was staring at
her and talking maliciously about her.

Isabel had put up but little fight. She lost Otto almost at once and withdrew herself into a sad, sarcastic

remoteness. Almost the last serious talk I had had with my brother, many years ago now, had been when I implored him, on his marriage, to get away from Lydia. I can recall the paralysed look with which he said that it was impossible. Shortly after that I departed myself. It was perhaps the spectacle of Lydia's ruthlessness to Isabel which finally sickened me and made me feel for my mother at last the positive hatred which was a necessity for my escape. Yet Lydia never destroyed Isabel: Isabel was strong too in her own way, another ruined person, but strong.

It was scarcely credible that all that power had simply ceased to be, that the machine worked no longer. My father had passed from us almost unnoticed, we believed in his death long before it came. Yet my father had not been a nonentity. When he was the young and famous John Narraway, Narraway the socialist, the free-thinker, the artist, the craftsman, the saint, the exponent of the simple life, the redeemer of toil, he must have impressed my mother, he must indeed have been an impressive person, a talented and perhaps a fine person. Yet my early memories are not of my father, but of my mother one day saying to us: Your father is not a good man, he is merely a timid man with unworldly tastes. We felt for him a faint contempt and later pity. He never beat us. It was Lydia who did that. He passed on to us only, in some measure, his talents. He had been a sculptor, a painter, an engraver, a stonemason. He left us behind, two lesser men, Otto the stonemason and I, Edmund, the engraver.

I looked at what lay before me with a horror which was not love or pity or sadness, but was more like fear. Of course I had never really escaped from Lydia. Lydia had got inside me, into the depths of my being, there was no abyss and no darkness where she was not. She was my self-contempt. To say that I hated her for it was too flimsy a saying: only those will understand who have suffered this sort of possession by another. And now the weird thought that I had survived her did not increase my being, but I felt in her presence mutilated and mortal, as if her strength, exercised from *there*, could even now destroy me. I looked with fascination upon the live, still burnished hair and upon the white, already shrunken face. Leaving the room, I switched the light off, and it seemed very strange to leave her there in the dark.

I moved softly across the landing to my own door. The house creaked about me as if in recognition, the inarticulate greeting of some primitive dog-like house-ghost.

I had no thought of waking Otto now. The closed doors breathed a stupefaction of slumber; and I wanted desperately to sleep myself, as if to appease with that semblance of death the angry defeated spirit. I reached my own door and opened it wide, and then stopped in my tracks. The moon shone clearly onto my bed and revealed the form of a young girl with long glistening hair.

For a moment it seemed like a hallucination, something hollow and incompletely perceived, some conjuration of a tired or frightened mind. Then the form stirred slightly and turned, the bright hair falling onto an almost bare shoulder. I started back and closed the door in a shock of guilty terror. This was a magic of exclusion which was too strong for me. A moment later, like an evil spirit put to flight, I was stumbling away down the stairs.

A woman's voice above me softly spoke my name. I paused now and looked up. A face was looking at me over the banisters, a face which I dimly, partly recognized. Then I realized that it was only my old nurse, the Italian girl. We had had in the house, ever since we were small children, a series of Italian nurserymaids; whether one had led to another or whether this was a foible of my mother's I never remember discovering. But one result had been that my brother and myself, with no natural gift for languages, spoke fluent Italian. The post had become, in a manner, traditional, so that I had always had, as it were, two mothers, my own mother and the Italian girl. Looking up now at the remembered face, I felt a sort of temporal giddiness and could not for a moment make out which one this was, while a series of Giulias and Gemmas and Vittorias and Carlottas moved and merged dreamlike in my mind. "Maggie."

Her name was Maria Magistretti, but we had always called her Maggie. I came back up the stairs.

"Maggie, thank you. Yes, I see. Of course, Flora is in my room. You've put me in Father's old room? Yes, that's fine."

As I whispered she pushed open the door of my father's room and I followed her into the bleak lighted interior.

I had never known her wear anything but black. She stood there now, a small dark figure, gesturing toward the narrow bed, her long bun of black hair trailing down her back like a waxen pigtail. With her pale, framed face, in the solemnity of the hour, she seemed like an attendant nun: one expected to hear the clink of a rosary and a murmured *Ave*. She looked to me ageless, weary: the last of the Italian girls, left, as it were, stranded by the growing up of her two charges. She must have been, when she came, but little older than the boys she was to look after; but some trick of fate had left her behind ever since in that northern house. Otto claimed he remembered being wheeled by Maggie in his pram, but this was certainly a false memory: some previous Carlotta, some Vittoria merged here with her image; they were indeed all, in our minds, so merged and generalized that it seemed as if there had always ever been only one Italian girl.

"A hot-water bottle in the bed? How kind of you, Maggie. No, not a meal, I've eaten, thank you. Just bed. It's at eleven tomorrow, isn't it? Thank you, good night." With this came to me some old comforting breath of childhood; warm beds, prompt meals, clean linen: these things the Italian girl had provided.

I stood alone in the faded, pretty room. The patchwork bedcover was turned back for me. I looked about. A lot of my father's pictures hung in this room, placed there by Lydia, who had, after his death, collected them from elsewhere in the house to make of this place a sort of museum, a mausoleum. It was as if she had, in the end, enclosed him in a narrow space. I looked at the pale water-colours which had once seemed the equal of Cotman, and the mannered engravings which had once seemed the equal of Bewick; and there emanated from them all a special and limited sense of the past. They looked to me, for the first time, dated, old-fashioned, insipid. I felt his absence then with a quick pathos, his presence as a sad, reproachful ghost: and it was suddenly as if after all it was he who had just died.

2 🕮 *Otto's Laughter*

Soft, sweet, mechanical, senseless music was being stereophonically produced. We were waiting for the coffin to be carried in. There was to be no service; only, as I gathered, a few minutes of quietness in the presence of the dead. Lydia had been a firmly convinced atheist. This was one respect perhaps in which my father had influenced her.

I had scarcely seen the family during the morning. Maggie had brought up my breakfast, and I had exchanged clumsy greetings with Otto and Isabel as we were getting into the cars.

I looked now at my niece, who was sitting a little in front of me on the other side, and savoured an astonishment in which last night's experience had some part.

I had not seen Flora for eight years, since she had not been at home on my last visit. I remembered her as a froward, exasperating little fairy, yet always to me infinitely gentle, with a spontaneous affectionate grace whose sheer directness seemed a miracle. She made nothing of the complicated barriers with which I had surrounded myself, and she loved me then, naturally and carelessly, just because I was her uncle, and accepted me utterly. She was perhaps the only person in the world who did. As a child she had wonderfully possessed that open, simple quality which makes adults oddly ashamed before children with a shame which is also a pleasure. Otto said I "idealized" Flora; but it was true that I might, for her, have come home often, often, if it had not been for Lydia.

But now she was, not quite grown up, but certainly a little girl no longer. She must be, I reflected, sixteen, perhaps seventeen. After all, I was over forty myself. And now she was beautiful. As a child she had had a broad, radiant, appealing expression and the sweetness of a little animal. Now there was before me a handsome, impressive girl, with long reddish hair, neatly pinned up, and a pale dreamy face in which the innocent radiance which I remembered shone like a surface mist above the firmer features of a grown-up. Her face had that pure, transparent look which we suddenly notice in the faces of young girls when they are no longer children. She wore a big longish striped skirt and a black tight-fitting jacket and a large black velvet broad-brimmed hat tilted far back on her head. She did not resemble her mother but had something of the gipsy grace of the young Lydia.

Isabel, beside her, looked morose and preoccupied. She too had changed, her face had aged in that imperceptible way, becoming yellower or greyer, as if a fine gauze of frowning and anxiety had been pressed upon it. But her mop of intricate brown hair was glossy and unfaded. She was smartly, quietly dressed and could have been taken for a clever businesswoman, a woman of affairs, while her face might have been that of a retired actress. She had a face which was in some sense old-fashioned, a round, rather wistful big-eyed small-mouthed face such as might have peeped and simpered at the turn of the century in some overfurnished drawing room in France. This appearance blended in a piquant way with her rather precise Scottish voice: Isabel came from the farther north, from north of the border. She caught my look now and half smiled. She had a good smile, that direct beam of one human being at another. I liked Isabel, though indeed I hardly knew her, and had often wondered why she had stayed on in that gloomy house, where she must have been so very far from happy. There was Flora, of course. And there are, I suppose, always for unhappy women many good reasons for bearing the devil they know rather than seeking the other one.

Otto I could not see, he was somewhere behind me, sitting with Levkin. That completed our party, except for Maggie, of course. Lydia had had, in latter years, few friends. I had scarcely spoken to Otto in the car, and I resolved now to have a quick business talk with him before lunch. There was no reason indeed why I should not get away promptly in the afternoon. Nothing detained me. I had not in the past enjoyed observing the wreck of my brother's marriage and did not imagine that I would enjoy it now. And though I was bound to Otto by steely bonds more awful than the bonds of love, we had, on our rare meetings, but little to say to each other. I wanted now chiefly to discover whether Lydia, who had been my father's sole heir, had left me anything in her will. It was unlikely, since after the scandal of my departure our relations had been cold, strained, and scanty. I gathered from Isabel that my name was never mentioned. Still, it was just possible that she had left me something, and I certainly needed it.

I lived a very simple and solitary life, but on the other hand I also earned very little money. The art of the wood-engraver may be deep but it is narrow. I passed my days contentedly with the twenty-six letters of the Roman alphabet, whose sober authority my father had taught me to love, combining their sturdy forms with wild fantasies of decoration to produce everything from book-plates and trade-marks to bank-notes and soap coupons. My father had frowned upon any decoration of the letter itself, whose classic familiarity he compared to that of the human form, and as a letterer I too counted as a puritan. I did occasional book illustrations, and for my own pleasure, with the names of Bewick and Calvert prayerfully upon my lips, transferred to the precious small surface of the wooden block many scenes, figures, objects that I saw or imagined. But I had never become a fashionable or well-known engraver and in that sense established. I was not ambitious. No type face bore my name. Perhaps I simply lacked talent. I had little curiosity about an exact estimate of my merits, and none at all about my prestige, except in so far as it affected money-making. I would have been happy enough to count myself a craftsman and to jog along in the background of some printing house, only a taste for freedom kept me at my own bench. I had no craving for luxuries and had never had, but I did not honour poverty for its own sake, and disliked its indignities and inconveniences. I lived a solitary life. It had not always been so. But my relations with women always followed a certain disastrous and finally familiar pattern. I did not need a psychoanalyst to tell me why: nor did it occur to me to seek the aid of one of these modern necromancers. I preferred to suffer the thing that I was.

There was a sound of movement, a shuffling, a heavy tread. As we all rose to our feet I half turned to see the little coffin entering, and it seemed suddenly sad that the hirelings who carried it so easily were equal in number to the real mourners. I shivered and closed my eyes as they passed me, and looked again to see the coffin reposing on a sort of stage in front of a blue velvet curtain. The music ceased, but continued in my head, making the silence idiotic. I looked at the coffin and sought for feelings but could only feel that I was cold, very cold. It was as if she were for the last time waiting, that so demanding spirit turned upon the threshold, and we were there in front of her, an embarrassed, pitiful, half-witted crew, hangdog as we had always been. At least a Christian burial would with ancient images and emotions have covered up this moment of blankness and lent to that querulous frailty the dignity and sadness of a general mortality. To this we all come. I wished, not for the first time, that I had been brought up as a Christian. Christianity was not inside me, for all that I sometimes aped it, and I knew the loss to be terrible. This was yet another thing for which I could not forgive my parents. I checked the old familiar resentment with the old familiar check. I stared at the blue velvet curtain. The silence went on and on.

Then suddenly, just behind me, there was a weird sound. I saw Isabel turning sharply and I turned too. The coffin-bearers stood stiffly in a row at the back. In front of them was the huge figure of my brother, and as I turned I saw him swaying, bending forward and putting his hand to his mouth. I thought for a moment that he was ill or overcome by tears: but then I saw that he was laughing. Monstrous giggles shivered his great figure from head to foot and turned, as he tried to stifle them, into wet, spluttering gurgles. "Oh God!" said Otto audibly. He choked. Then, abandoning all attempt at concealment, he went off into a fit of Gargantuan mirth. Tears of laughter wetted his red cheeks. He laughed. He roared. The chapel echoed with it. Our communion with Lydia was at an end.

The line of coffin-bearers was in scandalized disorder. Isabel had stepped into the aisle and was saying something to me. I turned towards Otto. But already David Levkin had seized him by the arm and was marching him, still gasping and rumbling, toward the door. As I left my place to follow them out I saw, behind Isabel, Flora standing perfectly still, almost at attention, gazing straight in front of her as if nothing had happened.

Outside, Otto was now sitting on the stone steps in the sunshine, repeating, "Oh God, oh my God!" and wiping his mouth with a filthy handkerchief. He seemed quite unable to stop laughing. He would stop for a moment, stare in front of him with a humorous delighted expression, and then, as if unable to endure the exquisitely comic nature of his thoughts, explode again into a roar. "Oh my God!" His eyes were running with water, and spittle foamed down his chin. Levkin was sitting on the step above him with his knee against Otto's shoulder. He was patting him with a patient, almost abstracted air. As I approached my brother I detected a strong smell of alcohol.

Drunkenness disgusts me. I recalled now that Isabel

had said in a letter some time ago that she thought that her husband was taking to drink: and I recalled how I had thought then that Otto, at best an uncontrolled and sometimes a violent man, would make a horrible drunkard. I looked down at him with repulsion.

"My Lord, my Lord, be quiet, be still." Levkin was speaking to Otto, singsong, caressing and soothing him. I looked at the boy with surprise and with an equal dislike.

"Let's get him to the car," I said. I detest scenes and drama. Fortunately there was no one about. The two cars stood but ten yards off, and beyond them the green trees of the Garden of Remembrance were resinous and sleepy in the sun. The women had not emerged from the chapel and our other attendants were not to be seen. "Get up," I said to Otto.

Levkin took one arm and I took the other and Otto rose between us like a giant log released from the sea bed. His face was now radiantly serene and he belched and hiccuped meditatively as we tacked and veered our way to the car. Levkin opened the door and Otto fell in. He smelt like an old bar parlour of stale drink and tobacco. I did not care to go on seeing my brother in this condition and it seemed kinder to him too to curtail the experience. "Take him away."

Levkin hesitated and then got into the car and began to turn it. The three women were now on the chapel steps. As I came back towards them I saw Isabel's face bent upon me with a look of apology and appeal.

Something in her eyes also said: This often happens, things are like this, do not make too much of it. Flora brushed past, tearing off her hat. "I'm going to walk home," she said brusquely to no one in particular. As she receded I saw her undo the pins in her red hair and let it fall down upon her shoulders.

"Come with us, Edmund," said Isabel entreatingly.

I felt at that moment that I simply wanted to shake them off like insects from my sleeve. Otto's laughter, Otto's reek of alcohol, the messy muddled personal smell of it all seemed suddenly to represent everything I detested. There was no dignity, no simplicity in these lives. In a few hours, thank God, I could leave them forever. "No, thanks, I'll stay here now. It's not far to walk back. Don't wait."

I watched the second car depart and then went slowly back into the cool chapel. It was not dark inside, plain windows and pale oak, but my eyes were dazed by the change of light and could not focus. Then I saw that the place was empty. Lydia was gone. The coffin must have receded through the curtains or sunk slowly into the floor, after the usual weird insipid rite of the cremation chapel. Lydia was in the furnace now.

I sat down and tried to compose my mind. I tried to think of her, to remember her goodness and her fineness, to remember how she had loved me and suffered for me. This was no moment for thinking of her frailty or for measuring her devastations. My petty judgements were put to silence in the presence of her mystery. I would study charity now, as I ought to have done before, as I ought to have done from the start. I tried to feel some remorse, a little sober regret for my own failure as a son, as a man. I must not flinch from a measure of that vast failure. *Nondum considerasti quantum pondus sit peccatum.*

These were the thoughts which I attempted to think, looking at the blue curtain beyond which my once-dear mother had passed. But I could not think them. All that came into my mind was the image of Flora. How exceedingly pretty she had become. I wondered how old she was.

3 ❧ Isabel Feeds the Fire

"You didn't bring your car?" said Isabel.

"No. I hate driving northward."

"Have a drink? Some whisky?"

Isabel's gramophone, turned down to an almost inaudible murmur, was playing Sibelius.

"No, thanks. I don't drink much." In fact I did not drink at all, only I always thought it sounded priggish and aggressive to say so.

"Unlike your dear brother!"

"How long has it been going on, the drinking?"

"Quite long, but especially since Lydia got so ill. Lydia was the only person who could control Otto. Thank you, Maggie, that will do. Just put the sandwiches on the table."

Maggie put down the tray and departed. With her neat black feet she seemed like a little donkey.

It was lunch time. Otto had not reappeared and Flora had sent news of a headache, so Isabel had suggested a sandwich lunch in her own room. She wanted to talk to me, she said, privately.

Isabel occupied the bay-window bedroom in the front with the view over the lawn towards the camellias. Our house, bought by my father on his marriage, was a big ugly Victorian rectory, its red brick darkened by the sour wind that blew from the nearby collieries, whose slag heaps were invisible behind the trees. In his young socialist days my father, who came from hereabouts, had chosen this little northern town in the hope of establishing fruitful relations with the working people. But the silent, suspicious miners had made nothing of that gentle personality; and by the time Otto and I were conscious of our surroundings he was already a defeated recluse. We grew up as children in exile.

The garden was immense and had been part of the grounds of a much larger house which had been destroyed by fire. A little mountainy stream of clear brown water spilled in over the far boundary in a long cascade, obedient to the will of some long-dead landscape gardener. The stream meandered for nearly a quarter of a mile between high slopes of camellias and dense thickets of bamboos before it briefly touched the lawn and turned away to flow under iron bridges into the town. The camellia bushes, indeed most of them were by now trees, unkempt and running wild, had grown into an almost impenetrable tangle of implicated vegetation. The course of the stream was marked by the greener line of bamboo, while high up above a birch grove led away into the open country. For us children it had formed a vast region of romance. I sighed. I could not remember being happy in childhood, but now it was as if the woods remembered it for me.

"No, thanks, Isabel, I don't smoke. I'm out of date about Flora. What's she doing now? I was surprised to see her so grown up."

"She's at the technical college, doing textile design. She has a small flair for it. I expect she'll get married young. She's longing to go south."

I sighed again. Through these various channels my father's big talent was gradually draining away.

"Thanks, Isabel, just one sandwich. You haven't anything soft, ginger beer? All right, tomato juice. What have you done to your hand?"

Isabel had a long pale scar across the fingers of her right hand.

"Nothing. I burnt it here on the grate."

"You must be careful with that fire. It's like a blast furnace. Surely you don't need it in summer?"

"It's company. Like a dog. I enjoy feeding it."

Lydia had always had a morbid fear of fire and kept at least six fire extinguishers in the house. Partly to annoy her, Isabel had always kept a very large open fire in her room, which she piled high with wood and coal. It was roaring away now, a dazzling edifice of red and gold, although the sun was shining brightly outside. Isabel took some drooping flowers from a vase and threw them onto the blaze. There was a sizzling sound and the room filled with a sweet pungent smell.

Isabel's room had always been something of a provocation. It was her hobby, doubtless her consolation. Whereas the rest of the house was still appointed in the narrowly fanciful style favoured by my father, a sort of Spartan *art nouveau,* Isabel had built herself a luscious and eclectic boudoir. The room was crammed with furniture and the furniture encrusted with objects, and my heavy tread on entering had set a myriad trinkets tinkling like little bells. It was an Edwardian room with dreams of the eighteenth century. I backed away from the fire and leaned on the end of the mantelpiece, carefully shifting some ivory water buffaloes out of reach of my elbow.

"Do sit down, Edmund. You'll break something if you go on loping around. You're much too big for this room anyway. Thank heavens Otto doesn't come here any more." She added after a moment, "Ah, you were so right to get away from Lydia."

Her voice with emotion became more Scottish. She was sitting now in a velvet sewing chair which was treading upon the toes of a Georgian games table and some ambiguous pieces of Chinoiserie. She must have changed some time after our return into what I had taken to be another dress but which I now saw to be a flowered summer dressing gown. She had thrust her feet into fluffy backless bedroom slippers. Since my last visit she had had her long hair cut off, though the elaborate curly coiffure had much the same appearance as before. Under the luxuriant hair her face was small, with little poised mouth and short pretty nose. She was thickly powdered, her eyebrows drawn in an exaggerated curve, and crude greenish smudges above her big round brown eyes. Below, her unpowdered neck, revealed by the open gown, looked gaunt and tired. I felt sorry for her.

"I'll stand if you don't mind. I always prefer standing. How are things generally, Isabel? How is Otto, apart from the drink?"

"All right, I suppose. He gets his work done. I never see him now. He sleeps in the workshop."

"I see he's got a new apprentice. I think you mentioned it in a letter. What happened to the last one?"

"Oh, he left early one morning with all the cash he could lay hands on and a lot of Otto's clothes. Of course Otto did nothing about it. Thank God Lydia was practically unconscious by then."

"What's the new one like? The same old style? Otto can certainly pick them! He seems foreign."

"Foreign parents, I imagine. Russian Jew. He lives in the summerhouse. I hardly see him either."

The summerhouse was a round stone building,

originally an eighteenth-century decoration, which later vandals had turned, with red brick additions, into a gardener's cottage. Yet it still looked pretty enough among the first trees of the camellia forest. Otto's workshop, an unashamed monstrosity of brick and slate, was happily out of sight behind the house.

"Where did he come from?"

"Out of the blue. He arrived the day Lydia had her last stroke. He has a sister or something with him. He hasn't done anything outrageous so far." She laughed her little laugh. Isabel had a tiny musical laugh which came out of her little mouth like a peardrop. She got up from her chair and minced, threading the furniture, to the window. "You make me restless. I do wish you'd sit down."

"Sorry, Isabel. I'm afraid of breaking a chair like I did last time. Isabel, do turn that music off, would you? I can't stand music in the background."

She leaned to switch off the gramophone. "I need music so much. I don't know what I'd do without it. Sometimes I wrap it round me like a wild cloak. Oh, Edmund, I've been so lonely."

I was a little nervous of the note of appeal in her voice. I did not want any display of Isabel's emotions. I had no wish to hear her confessions and complaints. In any case I knew it all but too well. I said briskly, "Come, come, there's always—" I was about to say "Flora," but felt suddenly that this might cause pain. I said "—the Italian girl."

"Maggie and I are like the people in Dostoevski who starved together in the hut for too long. We can do nothing for each other. Anyway Lydia took over Maggie as she took over Flora. She took everything."

"Yes, I can imagine she would have swallowed down poor little Maggie quite easily."

"There's a lot of Maggie left."

"There's a lot of you left. I'm surprised you don't get out more, do things in the town."

"Like *she* does. Maggie's quite a do-gooder. She knows all the Italian community. But I don't quite see myself as a baby-sitter."

"Surely it would help you to try to think about people other than yourself, other people's troubles—"

"You think I lead an idiotic self-centred life?"

I hesitated. There was an eagerness in her question. I did not really want to have this sort of conversation with my sister-in-law. Anything from me which savoured of rebuke would release some greater warmth into the atmosphere between us, and I shrank instinctively from this. I was, after all, only a passer-by. Yet I had to answer truthfully. "Frankly, yes."

My frankness gave her an immediate pleasure and she almost blushed with gratification. "You're quite right. My life is a *divertissement*." She moved from the window to the mantelpiece and began to drop dry shaggy bits of wood onto the fire. I backed away, edging my feet along the crowded floor.

"And you," said Isabel. "Yes, you lead a simple,

good life. You help people. Oh, I know about it. I wonder if you think it's easy to be like that?"

"I'm selfish too," I said. "It just suits me that way. I have unworldly tastes." I added, "And of course I had such an example before me in my father." I was beginning to hate the conversation.

"If only your father hadn't met Lydia! He ought to have been a monk. But in a way you're living his life for him."

"No one could live his life for him. He lived his own life. He was a much much finer person than I could ever be." Besides, I added to myself, I met Lydia too, and at a rather earlier age. I looked surreptitiously at my watch and wondered if my brother was sober yet.

"Yes, but you're a free man," said Isabel. "We are all prisoners here. We are like people in an engraving. God, how I hate engravings! Sorry, Edmund, but there's something about those black cramped things— it's a Gothic art, a northern art. And why do engravers always choose such gloomy subjects? Hanged men, wailing women. You can't be gay in an engraving. No colour. God, how I hate the north!" She tapped her wedding ring with exasperation on the mantelpiece.

I knew I was not a free man, but I was certainly not going to discuss this with Isabel. "There were plenty of Italian engravers. It wasn't all invented by Dürer. Mantegna, for instance—"

"Otto's Gothic, you know," said Isabel. "He is the

north. He's primitive, gross. Otto's the sort of man who'll pee into a washbasin even if there's a lavatory beside him."

I detest coarse talk in women and anyway would have thought it most improper to bandy words about my brother with his wife. I said in a cheerful leave-taking tone, "Ah well, Isabel, I think you are exaggerating. Even if you were imprisoned, you are much more free now. And you can be free at any time if you choose to be. And now, if you don't mind—"

"Don't be a fool, Edmund," said Isabel. She was pouring more whisky into her glass, and I realized with distaste that she was slightly intoxicated. "You know as well as I do that one can be imprisoned in one's mind. Here we've all been destroying ourselves and each other to spite Lydia. We've become monkey men and spider women. Otto and I are specialized destroyers of each other. Lydia's departure makes no difference to that."

The vehemence of her tone both touched and alarmed me. This was everything that I wanted to get away from. I felt compassion and yet knew that to be really moved by Isabel's plight would do neither her nor me any good. "Try and brace up, Isabel. Let cheerfulness break in occasionally! You can lead a happy, useful, independent life—"

"Do you remember," said Isabel, "how Saint Teresa describes a vision of a place reserved for her in hell? It's like a dark cupboard. Well, I live in that dark cupboard all the time. I am separated by my whole being from the good life you speak of. The only thing that consoles me now is sleep. Every night is an imitation of death. Without that I would have killed myself long ago."

She was tapping her wedding ring again, fiercely, her moist lips apart, her eyes wrinkled against the glow of the bright fire. She seemed dishevelled now, the flowery dressing gown pulled wide at the neck where she kept darting a nervous hand to rub her breast and shoulders.

In acute distress I turned to the window. Then, out in the garden, slowly crossing the lawn in the bright sunshine, I saw Flora. She had changed into a white summer dress and carried a big sun hat which she swung idly in one hand from a blue ribbon. Her hair was still undone. It was indeed not an engraver's task. It was a subject for Manet.

I exclaimed, "Why, there's Flora. How very pretty she is."

I could hear Isabel move behind me, and in a moment her sleeve was touching mine. We both watched the child as she strolled, head thrown back, as if she were aware of nothing but the brilliant trees and the bright, light blue summer air.

"Alice in Wonderland! She must be a joy to you, Isabel."

"Yes and no." She added half under her breath, "I wish I had other children."

Flora disappeared among the trees. I sighed.

"Still all alone, Edmund?"

"Yes." I moved away from her. My exasperated distress had gone, and in feeling sorry for myself I felt more sorry for her.

"How long are you planning to stay with us?"

"Well," I said, looking at my watch again, "if you'll excuse me, and if I can get hold of Otto now, I'll catch the five-o'clock train."

"*What?*"

Already halfway to the door, I turned to her. Her plump hands were crossed at her throat in an attitude of horror and supplication. "*No, no, no—*" she said. Then, with an air rather of authority than entreaty, she stretched out an arm in my direction. She seemed, in her golden fiery shrine, like a little prophetess. "You can't go, Edmund."

"Well, really, I—"

"You must stay. Something will hold you here. You must stay on now and help us. Otto needs you. We all need you. Who else could I have talked to like this? I was so much looking forward to your coming. You are the only person who can heal us."

"I am no healer," I said. I could not add: I cannot heal you. Perhaps no one can.

"Yes, you are. You are many things. You are a good man. You are a sort of doctor. You are the assessor, the judge, the inspector, the liberator. You will clear us all up. You will set us in order. You will set us free."

I was thoroughly alarmed by this speech. My intense desire was to return to my own simple, unencumbered place. I did not want to dally in the mess of Isabel's world, let alone to be assigned a role in it. I said firmly, "I'm sorry, Isabel. I don't exactly have to go, but I intend to go. I couldn't do anything for you and Otto. Now please forgive me and excuse me."

The tense prophetic little figure drooped, and she shambled back to the fire, knocking over a small table. One of the fluffy slippers had come off. She poured out some more whisky and said without looking at me, "Perhaps you're right, Edmund. You'd better get back to your good life. I shouldn't have bothered you like this. It's just that I'm caged, bored. I want emotion and pistol shots."

Emotion and pistol shots: Lydia had wanted these things too. They were just what I feared and hated. I fled from the room.

4 🌹 *Otto and Innocence*

"I dreamt last night," said Otto, "that there was a huge tiger in the house. It kept prowling from room to room and I kept trying to get to the telephone to ring for help. Then when I did get to the phone I found I couldn't dial properly because the dial was all made of marzipan. And then this tiger—"

"Do you mind," I said. "I do want to catch the train. And there are still various things to be settled."

We were in the workshop, and Otto was eating his lunch. The workshop, with large pieces of worked and unworked stone rising and receding about the central space, had a megalithic solemnity, like a meeting place of Druids. The stone seemed to give back a peculiar marmoreal quality of sound, melancholy and a little hollow, and to exude coldness. Otto now mainly produced gravestones and memorials. Sober plain surfaces of slate or marble recorded here and there in confident, impeccable Blado or Baskerville the names of the deceased, who could have no fears for their identity with their arrival in another world announced in lettering by Otto. A bright clear light from above showed the irregular whitewashed walls, now gauzy with innumerable cobwebs. A beautifully executed memorial tablet of dark green Cornish slate lay upon the workbench, where I had already noted with approval the neat, clean array of tools. Otto might be a mess in every other way, but he was still a meticulous craftsman. Our father had given us, in this respect, a training which could not be undone.

Otto was seated on top of his folded overcoat upon a long low marble tomb with his plate balanced on his knee. His lunch consisted of water biscuits, butter and cheese in great quantity, and, in a cardboard box beside him, a mound of herbs which he had plucked in handfuls from the overgrown herb garden. I remembered these tastes of his. Feeding Otto was like feeding an elephant or a gorilla. His great size required an immense bulk of green stuff per day. At this moment, with a pocket knife clasped in red bulging fingers, he was plastering on to a biscuit a piece of butter the size of a ping-pong ball; upon this buttery sphere a cone of cheese of equivalent mass was then balanced, and to the cone were made to adhere bushy sprigs of mint and marjoram which Otto seized from the pile of green fodder beside him, skilfully eschewing the pieces of grass, groundsel, ground elder, and other foreign greenery which the hastily gathered herbage was sure to contain. His gaping mouth remained open, revealing a green biscuity mess within, while he conveyed the greasy structure to it. Most of it got inside.

"Odd, isn't it," he mumbled, spewing out biscuit crumbs as he chewed, "that we are both practically vegetarians. I'm a vegetable man and you're a fruit man. I expect it's something to do with Lydia. Most things about us are!"

I was in fact a vegetarian, though by preference and on instinct rather than on any clear principle. I seated myself now upon the workbench, checking my usual tendency to pace about as I did not want to stir up the multicoloured stone dust upon the floor. I have a very sensitive nose. "Otto—"

"Gosh, I believe I've just swallowed a furry caterpillar! Poor little blighter. Will he poison me, do you think? I wonder what it's like to be eaten. Well, we should know. Oh my God!"

"Otto—"

"All right, all right. Things to be decided. Such as Lydia's tombstone, problem of. Christ."

"I leave that to you," I said. "Put on anything you like. I don't mind. And she won't mind now." We had had a discussion a little earlier about whether there should be any special inscription, and whether it should contain the words "wife" and "mother." They were words Lydia had detested. "Why not just her name, anyway?"

"Lydia. It sounds like a little dog."

"I mean her full name, you ass. Anyway, you decide."

"Funny, isn't it," said Otto, now cramming a leafy handful in, grass and all, "that I'm always so constipated, in spite of all the green stuff. Green seems the natural colour of food, doesn't it? Has it ever struck you that we don't eat anything *blue?*"

"Otto—"

"Have some whisky, Ed, or are you still on the wagon?"

"I'm not on the wagon. I just don't like the stuff. Haven't you had enough for today?"

Otto shook his head sadly, and when he could speak: "You just don't understand about addictions. One always wants more. The more one has the more one wants and the more frantically one wants it. Ah, if only I could give up the drink now. And just live blankly. Then one would really feel the hell one was in. It would enter the body." He paused, his mouth, full of green mash, wide open, and gazed immobile at the cobwebby wall.

I have said that Otto was taller than me. He was also wider and bulkier, his once bull-like frame turning to masses of fat. He still retained, however, an exceptional physical strength, and he was, when he wished to be, tireless. His face was enormous and had now become red and flabby. He had an absurdly short straight nose, a high wrinkled sweaty brow, tracts of soft pendulous cheek, and a wet shapeless gash of a mouth which usually hung open. Like me, he needed to shave twice a day, and, unlike me, he failed to do so. His hair, more plentiful than my own and still a dark mousy brown, fell longish, wiglike, very slightly curly round the dome of his head, so that he had sometimes the air of a middle-aged operatic bass. When he drew breath one might expect an organ-like boom; and indeed his voice was as loud, though not so musical. It was hard to believe we had resembled each other when young; possibly we still did in so far as a thin man can resemble a stout one. I had long stopped looking into mirrors, even when shaving. Neither of us had much of our father, another tall man but frail and elegant and pale as ivory, though I had been told many years ago that I was his image.

"It's just taken us in different ways, you and me," Otto was going on. I noticed that striped pyjamas were protruding from the ends of his trousers. This must have been his funeral garb. "You remember the thing father used always to be quoting, about the two birds on the tree, how one eats the fruit and the other watches and does not eat? Some Hindu thing. Well, you're the one that watches and I'm the one that eats. I eat and eat and drink and drink. I try to swallow the world. No wonder Isabel thinks I'm a sort of glutton-ous buffoon. Was Isabel complaining to you?"

"No," I said, "of course not." I was troubled by the quotation about the birds. I recalled my father uttering it, but I could not recall what it meant.

"Well, I expect she was, you know. God, if sarcasm and cool irony were grounds for divorce I could have escaped Isabel long ago! However, she has worse things to complain of. She finds me disgusting. I am disgusting!"

I wanted to keep off this. "By the way, I found a lot of fine boxwood blocks in Father's room. I wonder if I could have them if you don't want them."

"Oh, take them, take them. You may find they're a bit cracked, they've been there for ages. Isabel stopped me from engraving years ago. She said engravers made everything tiny, like looking through the wrong end of binoculars. Tinification, she called it. But that's just what *she* does. How right you were not to marry!" Everything led back to Isabel.

"That has disadvantages too!" I passed my hand over my lips. Otto is a wet-lipped man. I am a dry-lipped man.

"Only very carnal ones. The spiritual disadvantages of marriage are crippling. I could have been a good man if I hadn't married. Sometimes I think women really are the source of all evil. They are such dreamers. Sin is a sort of unconsciousness, a not-knowing. Women are like that, like the bottle. Remember that dreaming Eve at Autun, that dreaming, swimming, dazed Eve of Gislebertus? Ah, if I could have ever carved anything like that—but I'm good for nothing but provincial tombstones." He detached, with a big dirty hand, a flowery sprig of thyme and stuck it onto the cheese.

"You've done some very fine things," I said, "and you will again."

"No, no, Ed. I'm done for. God, if you only knew the mess my life is in! And it's not Isabel's fault, it's my fault, all my fault. *Mea maxima culpa.* Nothing redeems that central failure. And I can't even feel any proper regret about it. I'm caught in a machine. Evil is a sort of machinery. And part of it is that one can't even suffer properly, one enjoys one's suffering. Even the notion of punishment becomes corrupt. There are no penances because all *that* suffering is consolation. What one wants is not suffering but truth: and that would be a kind of suffering one can't even imagine now. That was what I meant earlier about giving up drink. If I could look with absolute blankness and truthfulness at what I am, even if I went on doing the same things, I'd be an infinitely better man. But I can't."

Otto was clearly still drunk. But a distant echo of my father in what he said touched my heart. My father had been a philosopher *manqué*. Otto too had his labyrinth, his metaphysical torture chamber. Indeed, I had my own. I understood Otto perfectly.

I said, "Work is one simplicity which can't be taken from us."

"You sounded just like Father then."

An old, old affection for Otto stirred within me. In a sort of fright I looked at my watch. I wanted to leave promptly and I did not want to be sorry to leave. I said, "Look, Otto, forgive me for rushing you. I've got that train to catch. Did Lydia leave a will?"

Otto stared at me, his mouth gaping, his eyes round and bloodshot. Then he said softly, "Poor Lydia is just dead and you are looking at your watch and speaking of wills." At such moments Otto could be frightening. I checked a movement of recoil. Then suddenly the tears welled out of his eyes and he bowed his big head into his hands. A red flush spread down his neck.

I was moved, more by a sort of pity for him than by anything else, but I remained cool. After all, I was the one that watched. I sat down on a block of Portland stone. "I'm sorry," I said. "I will mourn in my own way. I am not a public mourner."

Otto raised a wet crimson face. "I know, I know. You're a close one. You'll think it all out. But I just miss her." The tears came again.

I could hardly bear this. "Please, please, Otto. And don't worry about the will and all that. I shouldn't have spoken of it. I'll write. I think I'll go and pack now." In a strange and terrible way I missed her too. But I felt an iron intention to postpone my grief until I should have got back to my own house, where I could indeed "think it all out." Here it would be, somehow, too dangerous. I did not want to catch some last infection from the shade of Lydia.

"It's all right," said Otto. He was wiping his face with one of the rags he used to clean his chisels. "We may as well talk about it now. I haven't found the will yet. At least, Isabel hasn't found it, and she started looking as soon as Lydia had the first stroke. There may not be one."

"That wouldn't be Lydia, not to make a will. It'll turn up. It's probably somewhere in her bedroom."

"Well, maybe. Anyhow, she's probably just divided the property between us. There should be no problems. I'll give you half the value of the house."

"I should think it's more likely," I said, "that she's left it all to you and cut me out."

"I don't know," said Otto. "She and I rowed an awful lot these last years. You were the far-off hills. She might quite well have left it all to you and cut *me* out. That would be like her sense of humour!" He gave his orchestral giggle, stuffing the last handful of mint and dandelions into his mouth.

"If she has," I said, "of course I'll divide it equally with you."

"Well, I'll do the same by you if she's left it all to me."

It occurred to me that this arrangement was a bit unfair to Otto, since it was overwhelmingly more likely that if there was one heir it would be him. And after all he had put up with Lydia all these years. However, I decided to argue about that when the time came.

"Thanks, Otto. I suppose she'll have made some provision for Maggie?"

"I suppose so. If not, we will."

"Is Maggie going to stay here?"

"Of course," said Otto with some surprise. "Where should she go to? This is her home. She hasn't been to Italy for years."

There was a soft footfall and a figure emerged from behind a tombstone. It was Levkin, carrying a tray. I had not heard the outer door open, and it occurred to me that he might have been hiding among the stones for some time and listening to our talk. I did not trust any of Otto's young men.

The boy went to Otto, who gave up his plate and the greasy remains of his meal with the docility of a little boy obeying his nurse. Levkin packed the tray neatly. He looked at me with a slightly coy air, stretching his long neck like an animal, his big lips impudently pursed. He tossed his longish brown hair forward to veil his eyes as he leaned over, deftly removing the fragments of biscuit and cheese which had formed a milky way down the front of Otto's jacket. Then he removed a lump of butter from Otto's cheek with his finger, balanced the tray lightly on one hand, and stood springily to attention. "And when I get back, my Lord Otto, to work, yes?"

"Yes, David," said Otto. He hauled himself obediently to his feet with a grunt and a hiccup while the boy, with another humorous look at me, disappeared among the stones.

I was irritated. "Why do you let him address you in that idiotic way?"

Otto meditatively picked up a wooden mell and balanced it in his hand. "He's a good boy. And I think he's fond of me." Otto said that about all his apprentices, usually in the face of blatant evidence to the contrary on both counts.

I shrugged my shoulders. It was time to leave Otto and his problems behind. "Well, I'll be off."

Otto shambled after me. We climbed over a little suburb of marble blocks and opened the door. It had been cool and grey in the workshop with the clear northern light from above. The door opened upon the damp, sunny jungle of an English summer. Past one corner of the house, where the Virginia creeper hung like light-green cut-out paper upon the blackish-red brick, was visible a triangle of lawn seeming now almost golden in the sun. In the midst of this haze of gold Flora stood, as if she were waiting. She had put on her sun hat, and the blue ribbon was tied in a big bow under her chin. As the workshop door opened she turned and walked slowly away into the green shadow in the direction of the wood. We watched the nymph for a moment in silence.

"Innocence, innocence," said Otto. "To be good is just never to lose it. How does evil begin in a life? How *can* it begin? Yet we were there once—"

5 ❧ *Flora and Experience*

"Uncle Edmund, could I speak to you for a moment?"

I had left Otto behind in the workshop and was crossing the lawn. I had meant to give Flora a brief wave, not intruding on her summery solitude, and go to pack my case. Farewells could wait until, the taxi having arrived, they would have to be brief. However, on seeing me emerge, Flora had turned purposively towards me and there was no avoiding her.

"Hello, Flora. What a long time it is since we met. You must call me 'Edmund' now that you're so grown up, mustn't you?"

I felt rather awkward with her. She was not the little girl I had known, but she was not yet a woman either.

She seemed like some little ageless nymph of the woods, some gracious sprite from an Italian painting, too smooth, too slim, too luminous to be really made of flesh. I saw her as Otto had seen her, radiant with innocence, and I felt tongue-tied.

"You haven't looked at the stream," said Flora. "It's all different now. Do come and look."

"I haven't much time. But I'll come a little way." It would have been gross to refuse her.

As we went I heard again, from Isabel's open window, the sad music of Sibelius. Isabel was wrapped in her "wild cloak." I wondered if she was watching us now.

The trees at the edge of the lawn were mixed conifers and birches, very tall birches with long bare silver stems and high feathery foliage, looking more like eucalyptus than like the tamed birch of the south. Where the stream emerged and briefly skirted the lawn the trees drew apart to make an archway through which could be seen a shimmering of bamboos where the sun chequered the receding water course with a more golden green. It was a luscious miniature jungle scene such as would have delighted the eye of Henri Rousseau; and indeed, for all my anxieties and my sense of a great pain postponed, it took my breath away at that moment and I could hardly help seeing the distant pattern of the sharp bamboo leaves, framed by the birch pillars, as a fine subject for an engraving.

Of course it was a subject which I had done before; but as Flora had said, the scene had changed. We began to walk along the path by the stream.

The birches and conifers had receded here toward the top of the hill and their place was taken by the bamboos which fringed the water and the shrubby tangle of the camellias which clothed the slopes. The bamboos had invaded the stream now, their straight strong stems grouped in the water itself, while the stream, more choked than ever with its debris of round grey stones, meandered a blackish brown under the sun-tinged arches. The waterfall distantly murmured. A riot of wild flowers and grasses had covered the bank and made the path invisible and all but impassable. The jumble of campion and ragged robin gave place to briars and ground elder as Flora still pushed on ahead of me with determination in the green half-light.

The extreme beauty of the scene put me into an instant trance. It was always a trick of my nature to be subject to these sudden enchantments of the visible world, when a particular scene would become so radiant with form and reality as to snatch me out of myself and make me oblivious of all my purposes. Beauty is such self-forgetting. Yet in all this I saw Flora clearly, saw that her great-skirted dress was not white, as I had seen it before, but a very pale blue and covered with little black sprigs of flowers. Her heavy thick straight hair, still all undone, flopped and shifted on her shoulders like a garment, and as she stooped every now and then to detach some trailing stem from her dress, I saw her profile, her pale freckled cheek and strong, slightly up-tilted nose. The short upper lip and forward-thrusting mouth recalled my mother. But Flora's face was larger, heavier already in feature, and, it suddenly struck me, more modern. With that it occurred to me that Flora must be taller than either Lydia or Isabel. And then she looked to me less like Alice in Wonderland and more like a country girl painted in a truthful, unassuming moment by some honest, unambitious painter at the turn of the century. There was a certain simplicity, a certain unashamed prettiness.

I was brought to my senses by a large stinging nettle, which, in a leisurely manner, brushed itself lightly across the back of my hand, leaving behind a fine scattering of little red-hot pinpricks. I exclaimed and then called to Flora. "Look, let me come in front. What am I thinking of? You must be getting murdered by brambles and nettles. Or shouldn't we turn back now?"

I had half consciously assumed that the child was leading me somewhere. There was, indeed, at the end of the path, the cascade and the broad black pool into which it fell, a fine sight, and one which I had many times painted and engraved without ever producing more than an eighteenth-century pastiche. Perhaps the cascade really did live in the past. But the past was so thick with weeds now, it seemed pointless to continue. My coat was covered with burrs and little green pellets of goose grass, and I could see Flora carefully detaching her skirt from a bramble. "Let's go back, eh? I'm glad to have seen it. It's prettier than ever. We'll turn round and I'll lead."

"It's easier in a minute. We can get under the camellias."

I looked rather anxiously at my watch. I could, of course, catch a later train. I looked up and she had vanished. The place had me now under some sweet compulsion, and I followed. Next moment the green tangle was gone and there was bare dark brown earth underfoot.

The camellias, disciplined by the winds of severe winters, crouched on the slopes, rising here and there to the eminence of a tree, their branches and shiny dark green leaves twined and knotted into a continuous fabric. Underneath they formed a series of interconnected caverns or grottos through which, bending double, one could freely pass; and now I could see Flora's pale dress appearing and disappearing as she darted ahead of me under the low roof. With a sort of excitement I began to run too, bending very low to keep my head clear of the branches, and in a moment there was sunlight ahead.

When I emerged Flora was already sitting on the bank with her shoes off and her bare feet in the water. I was breathless, but she looked as if she had been sitting there all the morning. She pulled her dress up to her knees and looked up at me gravely.

My heart was beating hard after the doubled-up running. I must be out of condition, I thought, as I sat down beside her. Here the cascade seemed to make but little noise, a small music which surrounded us and seemed to form a shell in which the scene floated, detached and perfect. The cascade was not large, but it was so well proportioned to the pool that it seemed to escape the vulgar dimensions of real size and partake rather of the measureless nature of art. It fell from a shelf of rock straight into the round black pool and seemed to disappear through a foamy brown ring into the deep water, so little was the glossy black surface elsewhere disturbed. Above the rock the course of the stream receded up a green gully overgrown with bog myrtle and willow herb toward a birch-ringed glade at the summit. The sun shone on the pool but coldly, out of a bright pale northern sky. I looked up and was dazzled. Then I looked down. Flora's feet in the dark water were almost invisible. Her bare knees were a light biscuity brown, slightly polished.

It was easy to guess that this place was the child's private retreat. I could not see Isabel, with her high-heeled shoes, making the passage through the brambles, nor could I see the huge Otto crawling beneath the stooping camellias. Even as a child Otto had not been such a frequenter of the cascade. It had been my place. Now it belonged to Flora.

I rubbed my hand with a dock leaf until it was a green hand. Flora was picking white daisies from the bank and laying them out on her skirt. I thought it was indeed a pretty picture to take away with me. I looked at my watch. Then I looked back at Flora, at that smooth, unmarked young girl's face; and even as I looked I saw that she was starting to cry.

I was for a second surprised and at the next up-braided myself. After all, she had loved her grand-mother. Ought I not to be grieving too in just such a simple way? I still felt accused by Otto's perception that I would "think it all out." I said to her, "Don't grieve, Flora." Of course she must grieve. But "We are all mortal" or "You will soon forget her" could not be said to children, though both were true.

Flora shook her head violently, shaking tears off her cheeks. She was staring at the centre of the pool.

"It's not that."

"What is it, then?"

She turned towards me. Her face had become wet and red very quickly. It was as if she had whipped on a different mask. I looked with dismay at the puckered brow and the bloodshot eyes. "Uncle Edmund, do you really want to catch that train?"

"Edmund."

"Edmund."

"Yes, Flora. Or the next one would do. But I asked you what was the matter. Is it Lydia?"

The cascade softly encapsulated our voices in its sound, making a privacy.

"I said no. I want you to stay here and do something

for me." She had stopped weeping now and wiped her face, with the back of her hand. Darkened strands of hair adhered damply to her neck.

"What's the matter?" I was troubled by her wild look and by the solitude of the scene.

Flora then said something which I could not catch, or rather which I half caught and could not credit. "What?"

"*I am pregnant.*"

I stared at her. It was not possible. Then I felt a violent flush as if a warm cloth had been thrown round my head. I blushed with shock, with shame, and with an obscure and fierce distress. "*No.*"

"Yes, Edmund, I'm afraid." Flora was cooler now. She gently rubbed her face all over with both hands as if moulding it, leaving long green streaks. She looked down at her dark brown feet in the pool. "And you've got to help me. You've just got to. You're the only possible person. Are you terribly shocked?"

"No, of course not," I said. But I was shocked and horrified to the centre of my being. I could barely stop myself from shuddering.

"I think you are shocked. Father says you're a bit of a puritan."

This annoyed and sobered me. "But are you certain? One can make mistakes—"

"I'm quite certain now."

"Who is it? Who did this?" I found myself clenching my fists.

"That doesn't matter," said Flora. "It's a boy at the college. A boy called—Charlie Hopgood. But he's not important."

"I should have thought he was very important! Have you told your parents?"

"Don't bully me, Edmund. No, I haven't. Of course I haven't. I've only told you."

I tried to be calmer. I didn't want to seem to hector her. But I still felt full of the violence of the shock. "But this Hopgood knows, I suppose?"

"No—yes. He's gone away. He's nothing. Forget about him. I have to manage alone."

"Flora, Flora, I do think you should tell your parents about this."

"Don't be a fool!" The tears seemed suddenly to spurt from her eyes, falling all about upon her dress and upon my green hand. "You know my father. He would want to kill somebody. And Mother is useless. Oh, God, why ever did I tell you!"

"Child, I'm sorry. Please be calm. I will try and understand. But do you love this man? Would you want to marry him?"

"*No!* I've told you he's nothing. I'm telling you I'm in trouble and you've got to help me. Otherwise I shall kill myself. I can't swim. I shall drown myself in this pool." She hurled the little handful of daisies out onto the tense black surface of the pool.

"Don't speak like that! What can I do, Flora? Wouldn't it be better to be honest and—"

"You can find me a doctor in the south who would do the operation and you can lend me the money for it." She spoke fiercely and coldly, wiping her tears away. Then she withdrew her feet from the water and began drying them on the long grass. I saw her smooth brown legs and I felt her being utterly changed for me.

I stood up in extreme agitation. I felt as much horror and instinctive disgust at her pregnancy as if she had told me that she had some loathsome disease. Mingled with this was a moral nausea both at her plight and at its suggested remedy. And there was also, somewhere, a strong desire to find Mr. Hopgood and rapidly kill him. I tried to concentrate my attention on her last words.

I have very strong principles on the subject of abortion. It seems to me impossible to gloss over the fact that an abortion is a murder, the termination of an innocent life. How was I to convey this idea to the desperate young creature who had trusted me and asked me for such dreadful help? Yet it was my duty to try.

"You mustn't do it, Flora," I said. "You mustn't kill the child."

"You don't know what it's like, you men," she said softly, staring at the floating flowers. "I have this thing inside me, like a monster growing, growing. I hate it, I hate it. If it was born I should kill it. Why should I ruin my whole life at its very start? Who would want me, trailing round a beastly illegitimate child? I'm young. I want to have my youth and my freedom. I don't want a child now and I certainly don't want this horrible, horrible thing. Ah—you don't understand." She covered her face.

I said patiently, "It's not the child's fault, Flora. It is innocent. It might be a wonderful child and you'd love it. Remember, though it's such a tiny thing now, it's a human individual with a whole heredity, a whole destiny of its own. You would be destroying a whole human life. And think, if you had other children later, wouldn't you mourn then for this one and wonder what it would have been like?" I felt a fierce passionate desire to save the defenceless thing: all that innocence and purity which Otto and I had seen surrounding Flora like a halo was shrunk now into that pinpoint of being.

"Don't soften me," she said violently. "If you won't help me, go away. Go and catch your beastly train." She began to get up wearily, heavily, as if the child were already weighing upon her.

"How long a time?"

"Nine weeks. And I'm quite sure. I had a test. Well, good-bye, Uncle Edmund. Have a good journey. I'm sorry I bothered you." She brushed down her dress. "You won't tell them, will you?"

"Oh, Flora, Flora—" The first shock seemed now to have worn off, the horror was dulled, and I felt just an agonizing desire to help the child, to look after her. It was quite clear that I could not catch that train now. I would have to stay. "Flora, we must talk again about this when I've had time to think. I do want to help you. Of course I'll stay. And of course I won't tell them."

She looked at me more hopefully. We began to move back toward the glossy arches of the camellias. "Thank you, Edmund. I think I'll go and lie down now. I'm glad I told you. I won't see you till to-morrow and I'll try and think about it all. Come and see me early in the morning, will you? Come and have breakfast in my room. Eight o'clock. I always have breakfast there. What do you eat for breakfast?"

"Anything, Flora. Fruit. Anything. Yes, we'll meet tomorrow. And promise me you won't do anything foolish."

"I expect I'll do whatever you say," she said. "Only for God's sake look after me." She looked full at me with her streaked, tear-stained child's face and then stooped under the leaves.

I followed slowly, clawing my way along under the low branches. As the sound of the cascade sank to a murmur it seemed as if I had just come in out of a storm. I followed, with my head bent low, the flutter of Flora's pale blue dress, and I felt like a man under a yoke. Perhaps after all I should have to play the role which Isabel had designed for me. I wondered if I should prove worthy of it.

6 ❧ *The Magic Brothel*

A large dusky woman was holding a girl upon her
knee. The figures were mysteriously intertwined, the
wide draped knees seeming to belong now to one, now
to the other. Powerful arms reached out towards me
and I shrank away.

I woke abruptly from sleep and sat up, listening.
Something quite definite had awakened me. There was
a very faint hint of light in the room, the first light of
morning. I sat stiffly, like an awakened corpse, staring
at the unfamiliar window, while my heart raced, perhaps from the dream or perhaps from whatever it was
that had disturbed me. Then as the room made itself
known to me through the faintly grey darkness and I
recalled where I was and why, I felt disgust, almost

horror, at finding myself still in that house. I pushed off the bedclothes and sat on the side of the bed.

I was about to turn the light on but changed my mind. There had been some sound which I tried to remember, but my sleeping consciousness would return no answer. Perhaps some animal had got into the room, perhaps someone close by had spoken or called. It seemed foolish not to switch on the light, the dim scene was the very image of my alarm; but some instinct told me to hide, as if whatever it was were not yet aware of me. I rose quietly to my feet and listened again. The house was very still about me and yet alive, as if it breathed softly with the breath of sleeping women. I shivered and crept to the wide-open window. The faint dawn light, scarcely less than darkness, showed only the silhouette of the birch trees. The moon was down. The garden was totally indistinct. I leaned out a little and looked down into a grey obscurity of chill, damp misty air which baffled my eyes.

Then something appeared on the lawn. Something bright and coloured appeared in the middle of the greyness. I stared at the apparition with fascination and cold fright. I could not make out what it was or even where it was. It might have been on the ground or in mid-air. It moved a little, seemed to recede, and disappeared. Then a sound came, the sound, very low, a kind of moan or sigh, "Aaaah—" the sort of sound which someone might make when alone. The coloured thing reappeared, and I realized now that it was the light of an electric torch shining upon the grass. Beside it I gradually discerned the shadowy figure of a woman.

My first mad thought was that it was Lydia coming back to the house. Then I thought it might be Flora, Flora despairing, Flora running mad. But hazy as the form was, scarcely assembled in the dawn light, I knew that it was not Flora. It was someone else, someone unknown. I heard the sigh again, borne clearly on the damp, silent air, a little higher, a little louder, "Aaah." . . . Who was standing there alone and lamenting in front of the dark house, like a little figure in a dreadful picture?

As I looked I felt an alarming certainty that I was the only one who was wakeful. I was the only witness. I was the one who was summoned. Like a harbinger visible only to the victim, the woman had come for me. I donned trousers and jacket over my pyjamas and put on my shoes. I descended the stairs in darkness and fumbled with the chain on the front door. As I quietly opened the door I felt both hunter and hunted. To my alarmed relief, the figure was still there. I could yet have been persuaded that I had imagined it all; and it could have been, if it had disappeared forever, something much more frightening. I stood still in the shadow of the porch. There was more light in the sky.

She must have heard the chink of the chain as I opened the door. At some hundred yards' distance from me she seemed more still, aware of me. I could not see her face except as a blur. I began to move forward with careful footfalls onto the soft, weedy gravel and then onto the grass. I was compulsively quiet, frightened of another sound, frightened perhaps of a scream which should bring the house to life behind me with lights and faces. The woman did not stir, though I could see her looking at me. The silence continued.

When I was about ten yards from her I stopped again. I still could not see her face clearly, but she seemed to be young. She was wearing a long dress. A strong tension connected our two bodies. With a strange excitement I apprehended her fear, I awaited her cry, her flight. I wanted to reassure her, but the silence was a spell too great to break, and there was a weird, shameful pleasure in standing there before her, as if we were both of us naked. Then she shone the electric torch straight into my face.

I exclaimed, stepped to avoid it, and found myself very close to her. The torch went out and I saw that she had still not moved, indistinct, impersonal, and beautiful as a veiled girl. I had to speak now. "What are you doing here?"

I spoke softly, but the words seemed like thunder. She waited, as if for the echoes. Then she said slowly, "I have come to see the worms' dance."

Her stillness and now her strange words made me

feel as if I were still dreaming. She spoke with a foreign accent. I realized that the long dress was a nightgown.

As I stood beside her, dazed, my arms hanging, she said in an explanatory tone, "You see, here they are, so many of them."

She shone the torch on the ground. The lawn was covered, strewn, with innumerable long, glistening worms. They lay, one close by the other, crisscrossing the green dewy grass with their reddish wet bodies. The lawn was thick with them. They lay extended, long, thin, translucent, their tails in their holes; and as the torch came down, approaching nearer to them, they drew in their length and then whisked back into the earth with the quickness of a snake. I recalled this phenomenon now, which had greatly excited Otto in the days of our youth. The light was extinguished.

I said, "I hope I didn't frighten you. I am Edmund Narraway. And you—ah, yes, you must be—"

Then I saw that she was gone. She had vanished as if she had wrapped herself in the layers of morning light and become as gauzy as they. I thought I could hear her feet running. In a sudden frenzy of anxiety I began to run after her.

As I came among the faintly glowing birches and heard the crunching sound of my steps in the dry leaves I seemed to see the fleeing figure somewhere in front of me. The form of the summerhouse materialized among the trees with uncanny swiftness, and I had reached the door of it almost before I realized that she must have entered, recalled seeing or seeming to see her entering. I came up against the door in a rush. I was excited, startled by her sudden flight.

The door gave a little and then resisted me. I realized with a physical shock that she must be pushing against me from the other side. I paused and then said softly, "Please, please, please." The words, like words uttered in a fairy tale, seemed to change the scene and make everything resume its human shape. I stood back, and the pressure on the other side ceased. The door hung uncertainly between us, no more than a simple door that could be opened, the door of a human habitation. Then a light came on inside and the wood behind me was darkened as if night had returned to it. I went in through the door.

The summerhouse was originally a round building, a little green-domed Doric temple with merely a big empty space within. But later additions had given it an inner structure with two rooms up above and a kitchen annex below. Wooden stairs ascended from the lower space inside the door. The woman was standing on the stairs in the bright electric light. I blinked. It was indeed the next scene, and the hunter and the hunted had changed their masks.

"I'm sorry I ran after you—"

The light, falling from just above her head, seemed now too bright to see her clearly. She was wearing a long yellow nightgown with frills about her neck and about her feet. I had the impression that her feet were bare. Her hands were on her bosom and she panted still from her flight. Hair of a metallic copper colour, perhaps a false colour, fell almost to her shoulder, lank and straight. Her face, blurred in the sudden glare, seemed a dead white. She was young.

"You are David Levkin's sister?"

"Yes, I am Elsa."

I had almost completely forgotten Isabel's casual reference to a sister. Now it seemed I must have known who was the sighing figure who had compelled me to pursue her.

"Come upstairs." Her voice was dreamily expressionless.

I hesitated and then followed her up the wooden stairs, which creaked woefully under my weight. I saw the wet prints of her bare feet on the steps.

The first room upstairs had the air of a landing, with nothing in it except a huge oak chest and a ragged, sagging sofa. There was a strong smell of dust and mould. I stifled a sneeze. The inner door was closed. I faced her uncertainly, feeling both alarmed and dangerous. Slowly, facing me, she drew on a green dressing gown. The nightdress was not quite transparent.

She was a strange figure, tall, taller perhaps than her brother, with the same wide nostrils and the same full, heavy, sensitive mouth. Her lips were a moist scarlet and her eyebrows two thick black triangles, but her face was not otherwise made up and the skin was pale and waxen as if it would be cold and not quite human to the touch. Her metallic hair looked almost greenish now. Her eyes, round each of which was drawn a turquoise-blue pencil line, were so exceedingly dark that it seemed her hair must be dyed. They gazed at me, large and Oriental, the staring eyes of a sorceress or a prostitute, an artificial woman. I felt dazed, disturbed, confused.

I said in a low voice, "You mustn't let me intrude on you. I don't want to waken your brother. I was just surprised at seeing you and wondered—" I was going to say "why you were crying." But there were no traces of tears in those brilliant eyes.

"I often come," she said, "at night. You see, I am not allowed to go in the house. And it is this." Her voice was very foreign, and I could make nothing of her words; I was not even sure I had heard them right.

"Can I help you?" I said. The flight through the darkness and now her half-clothed nocturnal proximity, her curious animal calmness, produced in me an immediate elation, a sort of excited protective devotion. It was long since I had had so direct and yet so oddly natural an encounter with a woman. I felt ready to talk to her for a long time. And a sense that I might dangerously have taken her in my arms was instantly changed into a desire to serve her. Her tearless lamentation upon the lawn and now her mysterious words seemed like a sacred appeal directed especially to me.

She looked at me thoughtfully, as if taking seriously

what I had said. Then she said, "There is some coffee. But first I must show you something. After all, you are the brother. And we have waited for you a long time."

She moved toward the closed door of the other room and threw it wide open. There was already a bright light within, by which I saw, sprawled upon a low bed and lying half naked in the abandonment of deep sleep, my brother Otto.

The brightly lit scene revealed through the doorway had a crudely unreal quality, it was suddenly too large and too close, as if the girl had summoned up a gross simulacrum in a vision. Yet it was no psychological doll; it was indeed Otto who lay there displayed as on a stage, Otto open-mouthed and snoring, Otto huge, shaggy, deplorably and shamefully present and fast asleep. My first feeling was a curious dull sense of deprivation. Then I felt disgust and then a pang of guilt and fear. I feared my brother's rage should he awake and find me.

"He will not wake," she said, guessing my thought. "He has drunk. He sleeps like a pig. Come and see him." We went in together and she closed the door behind us. It was like entering an animal's den.

Most of the room was occupied by the divan on which my brother sprawled. Heavy curtains were pulled closely across the windows, and the atmosphere was stuffy and thick with a humid, pungent smell. The floor was covered with a mass of clothes which encumbered my ankles like sticky seaweed. A half-empty whisky bottle was standing upright in one of Otto's shoes. Otto, uncovered by the surge of the blankets, was wearing two very dirty round-necked vests rolled up in tubes about his chest, and a pair of equally reprehensible long woollen pants pulled well down upon his hips. His thick, soft waist was revealed, covered with a straggle of dark curly hairs, and below it the bare white protuberance of his stomach and the black cup of his navel, seemingly full of earth. His big bull-head was thrown back and his face seemed a crumpled mass of fleshy lines, his moist shapeless mouth ajar and gurgling. He seemed more like the debris of a human being than like a man.

The girl was staring down at him intently. Then suddenly she prodded him violently in the ribs with her bare foot. Otto groaned and settled his head more deeply into what I now saw was a pile of female underwear. The girl looked at me as if for approval of her demonstration, and said, "Elsa."

I found myself replying, "Elsa." The magical repetition of her name seemed like a charm which was to stop me from going away. She sat down now upon the bed and gestured me to sit too. Very cautiously I lowered myself onto the end of the divan, the odorous bulk of Otto rising and falling between us. And as I did so I thought again, in a resigned way, that if Otto were to open his eyes now he would probably break me in two.

I stared at the girl. She seemed solemn, cool, with a

pathetic air of tawdry ceremony. The aroma of whisky and sweat and sex from Otto was overwhelming; and I began to notice that she herself was far from immaculate. The pale, waxy, greasy face was very dark about the nostrils and smeared with blood and dirty about the chin. A downy moustache covered the deeply indented upper lip, and long fine hairs drooped at the corners of the full painted mouth. Her hands, busy now at the neck of her nightgown, had long chipped nails, patchy with old polish, and I saw that she was wearing a number of what appeared to be diamond rings. The metallic hair fell wantonly forward to veil the big, crudely outlined exotic eyes. I found her extremely attractive. I was filled with a repulsive excitement and shame and glanced down at Otto. He slept, his open mouth like a wet red sea anemone.

"You are Edmund from the south. Will you have some whisky?"

"No, thank you."

She picked up the bottle from Otto's shoe and tilted it to her lips, closing her eyes. "You know my brother David. Do you like my brother? We are Russian Jews."

"Yes, I like him. Where do you come from in England?"

"We are not of England. We are of Leningrad."

This surprised me a little. I had seemed to gather from Isabel that the Levkins were only of distant

Russian extraction. "Have you been over here long?"

"Since six years."

"Why did you leave Russia?"

"It was my father. We were young then. My mother is since long dead. My father was a piano player, he is very grand, very much known, but he cannot like Russia because it is not good for the Jews. He laughed at the synagogue, but in his heart not. In his heart he is always very sad. Then one day he took us through a big dark forest and we walk and walk and then there are such big wooden towers and bright lights and we run and run and they are shooting at us—"

"But you all got through—"

"My father was hit in the hand with a bullet so that he cannot any more play the piano ever."

"Ah—I'm sorry. Where is he now?"

"He is not anywhere. He is dead of what they say is a broken heart. So after that we are wandering people. You see these rings? Before my father die he give to us these diamonds so that we are not poor in whatever country we are. They are of very much value but we do not sell them because they are remembering of him."

She spoke in a casual singsong voice, as if she had told the story in just those words many times before. She had lifted her hand now and was flashing the diamonds about in the light. She seemed less a victim than a little lost princess telling an ancestral legend in a strange court. Yet I pictured the scene at the frontier, the terrified fleeing children, the father's wounded hand. It was no legend but a tale of today, an everyday, everyman tale. I began to tell her, to tell them all, that I was sorry.

But now for the second time I saw that she had fled. She had drawn her knees up and thrust them into the crook of Otto's knees and fallen down beside him. Perhaps the memories had been too much. She closed her eyes and seemed to go instantly to sleep. Otto moved slumbrously at her contact and for a moment the two bodies quivered and shifted in sympathy before settling down conjoined, her head against his neck, her knees within his knees, her hand in his hand. They looked unbearably, cosily conjugal. I stared at them for a while, Adam and Eve, the circle out of which sprang all our woes. I stared at them until they became a mere pattern of lines, a hieroglyph. I covered them with a rug.

7 🪶 *Two Kinds of Jew*

"So you have discovered the lovebirds!"

David Levkin was standing at the door. As I moved hastily away from the bed he passed me and pulled the curtains wide apart. It was bright daylight and a sunny morning.

My one thought was to get out of the summerhouse as quickly as possible. I shot out of the bedroom door, practically leaped the stairs, and came out into the cool wood, where the sun was streaking the birch trunks with a pure and scarcely spotted white. I felt I had waked from a bad dream. I took a few paces down the path.

Someone touched my arm and I found that Levkin was following me. I felt irritated and absurdly guilty at his having discovered me watching the sleeping pair. I walked faster and he still followed a pace or two behind. He touched me again.

"How did you know about them?"

"I didn't know about them. I heard your sister out on the lawn crying, and I followed her."

"Yes, she goes often at night. She thinks that she is a ghost, to haunt the house. But she is not sad. I think she suits your brother. Is it not so?"

"It's nothing to do with me." I kept walking on, not looking at him.

"But it will be to do with you. For you will stay with us now? You will stay and help us?"

"Go away," I said. I loathed his tone of voyeur-like complicity. I wanted to forget Otto and his greasy enchantress, they were no business of mine.

"They sleep well, don't they? You could watch them all night. It is the drink, I believe. Was my sister long asleep? Do you think she is beautiful?" He plucked at my sleeve again.

I turned to face him. "Levkin, I have no wish to discuss with you the affairs of my brother or your sister."

"The affair! The affair!" he said excitedly. "And my name is pronounced Lyevkin, Lyevkin. It means 'little lion' in Russian, and I am called that. At least you may say it means so, for, you see, a lion in Russian is *lyev.* . . ."

I walked on. He followed and then started chattering again. "Isn't it a beautiful day, Mr. Edmund? A fine clear morning. I love these mornings when I come over to wake them. So beautiful. A philosopher says it is our greatest crime, to ignore the beauty of the world."

"Clear off."

"May I show you my paintings, Mr. Edmund? I work as a stonecutter. But really I am a painter. And you too are a painter—"

I stopped and faced him again. There was something menacing and unpleasant about all this chatter, and I wondered if he was putting on some kind of act. I disliked his glee over Otto's situation, and it distantly occurred to me that he might be intending blackmail. Blackmail would be just in the style of Otto's apprentices.

"I'd advise you to practise keeping your mouth shut," I said. "Otherwise you'll find yourself in trouble. You haven't been long enough in this country to be able to take any chances. I don't suppose you've even got a British passport." I thought it would do no harm to frighten him a little in a vague way. I was alarmed for Otto, and I did not trust that boy with his air of a merry little procurer.

Levkin's response was surprising. He gave a wild burst of laughter, doubled himself up with glee, and then sprang high into the air. "See," he cried breathlessly, "I lev-itate, I lev-itate!" He paused in his gyrations, viewed my grave face, fell to laughing again, and gasped out at last, "Whatever did she tell you?"

I was bewildered. "Well, she told me how you had come here—"

"Oh, which one, which one! I can hardly bear it!" He held his stomach for laughter.

"What do you mean, which one?"

"Which story was it this time? The story of swimming the river, or the story of the aeroplane, or the story of the tunnel—"

"She said you came through a forest—"

"And our poor old father's hand was hit by machine-gun bullets so that he never played the piano again and died of a broken heart?"

"Well, yes—"

"And the rings, did she show you her rings, how they were diamonds my father got for us?"

"Yes—"

"Oh, how funny she is! She tells so many different stories, and they are all false. That one is just now her favourite. She read it in the newspaper, about the poor man's hand. No, no, Mr. Edmund. We are not such romantic people. My poor sister is a little fanciful, I'm afraid. Our father is not a pianist, he is a merchant of furs, and he did not die of a broken heart but is very much alive and making his money still, and we were not born in Leningrad or wherever she said, we were born in Golders Green. And as for those rings, they are rings of glass which she has bought for a few shillings. So you see how wrong you are to threaten me, Mr. Edmund, for I am as British as you are—and indeed I mean no harm, as you will see when you know me better and we become friends."

"I doubt if that will happen," I said. "But do I understand you—your sister—perhaps imagines that all those things happened?"

"Yes, she is a little—not crazy, quite, but, as I say, fanciful, she imagines, yes. She has what we call *Polizeiangst*. She thinks always she is persecuted. Did she tell you of the little men in this wood who are watching her? No? She is so troubled by being a Jew. She suffers it all the time, and all what is happening in all the world to Jews, she thinks that it is happening to her."

"Poor child," I said. I recalled the waxen face and the staring eyes. Yes, a little mad, perhaps. Another victim of a wicked world. I let Levkin lead me along a path that led away from the house and went by a roundabout way to the workshop.

"She is a witch, though," said Levkin. "A *rusalka*, as they are called in Russia. She has a sort of death in her. And she is fallen, oh, fallen ever since she is very young. She has had many, many men. That is what Lord Otto likes. That she is crazed and that she is a prostitute. And she likes him because he is a monster and a ruin. But I should not talk like that about my master, should I?"

"No," I said, "and now—" In fact I was interested in

what he had said and extremely haunted by the tattered image of the poor deranged girl. I could indeed understand what might fascinate Otto here.

"You see, there are two kinds of Jews," Levkin went on, walking very close just behind me. "There are the Jews that suffer and the Jews that succeed, the dark Jews and the light Jews. She is a dark Jew. I am a light Jew. I will work, I will succeed. I will succeed in art, or else in business, perhaps in art business. I will earn enormous money. I will not remember. I will not remember anything. She is all memory—she remembers so much, she remembers the memories that are not her own. She thinks she is the other ones, the ones that suffer and die. So she will suffer, so she will die young, I do fear it. But I will leave all that. I will levitate myself in the world. I will live in the world of light."

"How long has this been going on, with my brother?"

"Oh, long, months and months, since we are here."

"Does anyone know except you?"

"Wait, wait, Mr. Edmund. Do not walk so fast. No, no one knows, no one but me."

"Well, keep it so," I said. "Good day."

We had now reached the edge of the garden and I turned from him quickly across the lawn. The sun had dried the dew. The worms were gone. I felt disturbed, exhilarated. I wanted to think about what had happened to me. Yet of course it was no business of mine. I did not belong here, I was going away soon, perhaps that very day—and with that I suddenly remembered Flora. I looked at my watch and could hardly believe my eyes. It was after ten o'clock. I began to run towards the house.

It was suddenly incomprehensible to me that I could have simply forgotten my rendezvous with the child. I had been, when I went to bed last night, so full of it, I could think of nothing else. Yet somehow the weird night scene, the crazy princess, and the delinquent Levkin's chatter had so seduced and absorbed my imagination that what was most important had gone quite out of my head. I ran into the house.

Flora's room was my old room. I ran to it with pounding steps, shaking the place. Surely she must still be there, waiting. I knocked quickly and opened the door.

The little desk-table was laid neatly for breakfast, with two plates and several bowls of fruit: apples, bananas, oranges, apricots. There were also bread, butter, Swiss cherry jam, and a big jug of milk. Flora had laid it all out with loving care. But she herself was gone. I came in more slowly. There was a note propped up on the table. *I waited and you did not come. F.* I sat down heavily on the bed, utterly horrified with myself.

I looked up and saw someone looking at me. "Oh, Maggie—she's gone. You say she looked for me everywhere? The bus, just before ten, of course."

The Italian girl looked at me with the distant air of a

servant and a familiar, with an unsmiling, impersonal reticence. The grave undemanding face, the anonymous black dress, the trailing bun of hair: nothing could be more unlike the place where my imagination had just been roaming. She came forward and began to put Flora's little breakfast onto the tray. I slunk from the room.

8 🌹 *Otto Confesses*

"I dreamt last night," said Otto, "that there was a sort of big snake in the house. I could hear it slithering from room to room after me, and I was running to get to the telephone. I closed the last door against it and tried to telephone the police. But the dial was full of insects, and wherever I put my finger there were quantities of beetles and woodlice, and I couldn't dial properly without crushing them. So I didn't dial, and then this snake—"

"Where's Flora gone?"

"I've no idea," said Otto. "Has she gone? I imagine she's gone back to college. She's so casual with us now, she just comes and goes as she pleases. You'd better ask

Isabel. In my dream, the woodlice were the kind that roll up, and—"

"Otto, last night—"

"Yes, I know. David told me."

I had searched for Flora in vain. I had taken the next bus to the railway station, I had telephoned the college, the hostel where she usually stayed, I had even asked for Mr. Hopgood, but no one at the other end seemed to have heard of him. In fact I had little hope of tracing her: she had run away, she would hide. She had said that she would do what I told her, she had asked me to look after her: and at the crucial moment I had allowed my mind to be too full of other things. It seemed to me that I had undergone some sort of dubious enchantment, I had been, almost as if purposely, captured by magicians. Yet I knew this was but a false excuse. If my heart and mind had been sufficiently full of Flora and her needs I could not possibly have forgotten to look at the time. I knew too that the scene in the summerhouse had excited me extremely. I was affected by some old sense of the connection of Otto's life with mine, a sense of our being, though so dissimilar, identical. I but too perfectly understood the attraction to which my brother had succumbed. I felt pity, and yet I also felt myself degraded, tarnished.

It was also now clear that I could not go away. I was a prisoner of the situation. Earlier in the day, wandering in a state of aimless lassitude, I had been sharply tempted to depart. Flora was gone, Isabel was lying down and would see no one, Otto was still immured in the summerhouse. I felt awkward, alien, excluded. There was nothing I could do for these people. Yet, ardently as I desired to go, and even as I advised myself to return to my simple world before something worse should happen to me, I knew I could not. It was my duty to stay: that harsh word riveted me to the spot. But it was not only that. I realized with alarm that I *wanted* to stay. I was becoming myself a part of the machine.

It was then that I decided I must speak to Otto about last night. The brother and the sister would probably have told him of my apparition. But I felt that I must, if I was in any honesty to remain, have it out with him myself. I decided this in some trepidation, for I knew how sudden and how violent Otto's rages could be. I had of course no intention of telling him anything about Flora. I could not even decide to speak of that to Isabel. I kept wandering about and visiting the workshop until Otto appeared there, very dishevelled, about five o'clock. I conjectured how he had spent the afternoon. I found that I could not help being curious, though I disliked the curiosity and hoped it would not be too evident to him.

I had come in to find Otto opening a bottle of whisky. He had filled a glass jug with water from the water butt and was gloomily inspecting the brownish liquid, in which various small animals were swimming round. He carefully poured some of the water into a glass, trying to retain the animals in the jug. It was not easy. He then filled the glass up with whisky and sat down on a bale of packing straw. The bale sank abruptly in the middle, leaving Otto sitting almost on the ground, lying back cradled in the straw. He looked helpless, like an enormous baby. I sat down on some blocks of Westmorland slate.

"Yes, David told me," said Otto thoughtfully, staring at his muddy drink. He sighed and drank some. "The trouble about becoming an alcoholic is that ordinary states of consciousness are simply a torment. I suppose that *is* being an alcoholic. You keep off it, Ed."

"I do." I decided to let him pursue the matter if he wanted to. I could see him debating, looking at me, looking back to his drink. The long woollen pants emerging from his trousers camouflaged his dusty boots. His dirty shirt was open at the neck, revealing the familiar vests. Isabel must long ago have ceased to interest herself in his wardrobe.

"So you saw my *malin génie*."

"Yes." I could think of no comment on her. She had fascinated me. But there was little point in telling Otto that. I added, "Levkin said—no one knows."

"He exaggerates, as usual," said Otto. "Isabel knows *something* is up, I suppose. I think Isabel just tries not to think about me. So she doesn't bother about the details. And the Italian girl must know; she's not an idiot. Flora doesn't, of course, thank God, she's been away."

"Did Lydia know?" I suddenly could not imagine Lydia tolerating anything of the sort; and the curious pain which the discovery had given me changed into a mourning for her. She was gone indeed.

"No," said Otto slowly. "You see," he said, "I did try very hard to stop. I can't explain this thing to you, Ed. You probably think I'm mad. But it's like nothing I've ever known. I've never had a really complete, absolutely perfect physical relation with a woman before. You may think I'm a poor fish for that, but it's the truth."

I had myself never had anything approaching a perfect physical relationship with a woman, but I was not going to tell Otto that. I said, "And this is—very good?"

"It's a miracle. It's completely changed me. My whole body. I know I look like the wreck of the *Hesperus*, but I feel radiant, as if I had an angelic body. While with Isabel—well, Isabel always made me feel I was disgusting. With her I *was* disgusting, I was a pig, I felt unclean. With Elsa—everything I am and do is beautiful. Oh, I can't explain. But—"

"But you feel guilt?"

"I suppose that's it," said Otto dubiously. "After all, we are puritans." He drank up the whisky and floundered in the straw, trying to reach the bottle. I passed it to him. "Passion is its own excuse. At first there wasn't any time for guilt, any place for such a thought. And I made her so happy. I was on my knees with gratitude every day. It seemed so good, so *human*. But then, when Lydia got very ill—"

"It was more painful to—deceive?"

"Not just that. I deceived everyone cheerfully at the start. No, it was deeper. I could not go on making love when Lydia was dying. I felt I wanted to disown my body. It was a dreadful sort of physical torment. Oh, Ed, you were lucky not to see Lydia dying. She didn't want to, you know."

I preferred not to think of this. "So you tried to break things off?"

"With Elsa, yes. And it wasn't only Lydia. Of course I was scared stiff of Flora finding out, it could do her such awful damage. But it was Isabel too in a funny way. I know Isabel and I ought never to have got married, we're about as unsuited to each other as two people could possibly be. But Isabel's stuck by me, in her way. She's got a sort of—brave dignity. I don't know if you understand me. Lydia was such hell to her. And this thing has become such a *mess;* and if one starts thinking in terms of the future, it has no future."

"You wouldn't think of marrying Elsa?"

"Good God no!" said Otto violently. "I want with Elsa just *that*. And it's not just lust, it's good, it's beautiful, for both of us, it's something in the truth. I'd always really felt sex was wrong—but not with her. I feel I'm, in that way, in the truth for the first time in my life. I married Isabel with a hundred lies in me, and it's been worse since. This thing with Elsa was like a sort of redemption, a wonderful return to the beginning. But you see it's no good, it's doomed. There's no place for it, I can't go on living it, it's not eternal, it has to have a beginning, a middle, and an end. There isn't anywhere for me to *go* with Elsa, there's no road. And as soon as I realized *that* I felt I ought to stop it. I expect you think I'm simply justifying a piece of bestiality—"

I was far from thinking that. I thought I knew what Otto meant about being "in the truth." I had never, in anything directly to do with sex, been anywhere near that truth myself. "No, no. But I can understand that once you clearly put it to yourself that it had no future — After all such things can't last—" I felt very sorry for Otto and grateful to him for talking to me frankly.

"And yet, you see," said Otto, "how can I leave her, how *can* I? The thing is both essential and totally impossible. I tried to break things off in the spring— well, I did break them off. But I never really explained anything to her. And she sort of accepted it because she thought it was temporary and just because of Lydia. But now—I can't announce to her that she must go, I *can't*. And now it's all beginning to be poisoned. The innocent time is over. And yet it still gets stronger every day, the bond, the chain, the machine. I'm terrified that she'll begin to feel, to be, my vice."

"The dreaming Eve of Gislebertus—"

"Yes. I spoke of that, didn't I? It was really her I meant, Elsa. I know she's an innocent being, and I say that although I know what she did before she met me. I know she's innocent, and yet she sometimes seems to me the incarnation of pure evil. I'm sorry, this sounds mad. I know it's my own evil, of course, that I project out onto her. But I do see her as a demon. 'But to the girdle do the gods inherit—' I know it's something to do with my own horror of sex and my own real beastliness—but there are moments when I could positively kill her." Otto was shaking, his eyes goggling, his jaw trembling. His mouth pullulated in his face like a live animal. He struggled up to a sitting position in the straw, spilling the whisky over his jacket.

I felt nervous for him, of him. I was afraid he might even now break down in some alarming way. I was deliberately calm. "Is she really so deeply attached to you? When you say you *can't* leave her—"

"Oh yes, she loves me," said Otto. "I think I'm the first thing she has really loved. Perhaps she can only love a sort of Caliban. And I am father, brother, son, lover to her. But it isn't only that. I pity her so much. I am so very sorry for her. And that somehow makes it impossible for me to abandon her. Whatever would she become? And I cannot bear her tears, they are intolerable. I pity in her the whole world's sorrow, somehow."

"You could pity that in anyone," I said rather impatiently. "You pity her, and yet she is—your vice?"

"These things are very closely connected, you know," said Otto. "Desolation, dereliction, muddle, sin. I can't reach her sort of despair because when I pity her I despise her. I suppose again it's really something in myself. I feel myself victim, muddler, sinner all in one. Ah, if I could only separate these things! That's what I meant about giving up drink."

"To suffer, but purely, without consolations?"

"Yes, to suffer like an animal. That would be godlike. But one can't. 'For who would lose, though full of pain, this intellectual being, those thoughts that wander through eternity. . . .' It's the wandering thoughts that are the trouble. It was a fallen angel who said that."

"Properly, I suppose, one should suffer like an unfallen angel. But perhaps you are right, animal suffering is the nearest our imagination can get to that. But you are metaphysical, Otto. You ought to think about her in more simple terms. She is, isn't she, a little—odd?"

"You mean deranged, crazy. I can't think of it so. She seems to identify herself with others who suffer and she does it so intensely. She does sometimes say odd things, David has told me things she's said. But it's not like madness. It's more as if we, who don't do that, are mad."

"You say Levkin told you—but haven't you talked to her yourself?"

"Well, no, we don't *talk* exactly. Well, yes we do, we make jokes."

"Oh. Do you trust Levkin?"

"Yes, of course. He's devoted to me."

"Mmm."

It was darker now in the workshop. The big sky-lights above were an intense evening blue, but the light within was already golden brown, making at once more vivid and more uncertain the receding forms of the stone city. I could not see Otto's face clearly. With a great thrashing of straw he scrambled up and stood, his clothes covered in yellowy wisps, his arms hanging limply, his head jutting, like an untended marionette rather precariously standing upon its feet. One expected him at any moment to crash over one way or the other. I stood up too.

"Ed, would you do something for me?"

"Certainly, if I can."

"Would you talk to Isabel?"

I was surprised and rather dismayed. "What could I say to her?"

"Oh, anything, you know. She respects you so much. She must know *something* about this business. And I'm terribly oppressed by the feeling that she—doesn't understand."

"I doubt if I could make her understand," I said grimly.

"Well, no. But I'd just like to feel I was sort of connected with her again."

"But, Otto, you can't be—exactly—just now. And anyway any connection that remains between you two is nothing to do with me or any other outsider. I might only do harm."

"No, no," he said obstinately. "You would do good, good. Someone like you can't help doing good. You'd console Isabel, you'd cheer her up. And I do want her to know that I'm not such a total monster. Sometimes I think she might just run off."

I was touched by this; though I felt that today's talk had provided me with but scant material for purposes of impressing Isabel. "I'll talk to her a bit if you like. But I'd rather talk in—well, general terms. I see no point in trying to explain you to Isabel, especially just now!"

"Yes, yes," said Otto. He seemed pleased and swayed enthusiastically to and fro as if someone were now agitating the strings. "In general terms. That's right. In general terms. You are so good at talking in general terms. You'll help her."

"I wish I could help *you*," I said, "but I can't. Perhaps we're missing our religious upbringing." I prepared to leave him.

"It would have been a delusion," said Otto. "It's not punishment, it's acceptance of death, that alters the soul. That *is* God. And of course no organized religion will tolerate it. I shall continue in my muddle. Thanks all the same."

9   Edmund Is Tempted

"Well, and how much has our inspector found out?" asked Isabel, poking the fire vigorously. The logs turned on their backs, revealing golden bellies, and a fierce stream of sparks roared up the chimney. It was late that evening.

"Everything, I should think," I said gloomily. And more than I shall tell you, poor Isabel, I thought.

I could still not decide whether to speak to Isabel about Flora. It was unlikely that Flora would have gone to any place where she could be found by her parents. I had promised solemnly not to tell, and that promise was my last link of good faith with the child. I did not want uselessly to jeopardize any power I might have to help her later on. For the moment at any rate I thought I would keep silent. But I felt very troubled and hoped that the morning would bring some news.

"Ah, not everything," said Isabel. "I'm sure not everything yet. But keep on. It'll all come up to the surface, stinking like mad." The gramophone was playing Wagner, but so softly that the quiet parts were inaudible and the loud parts were a sort of crackling buzz.

I had intended to wait until the morning before carrying out Otto's request, but I felt restless and worried about Flora and I simply needed company. Also I was, in a rather disgraceful way, a little curious to see how Isabel would react to the "general remarks" which, as I entered her room, I had certainly not thought out.

Except for a dark-shaded lamp in a far corner, the room was lit only by the fire, which threw great waves of light and shadow across the scene. It was, I thought, dreadfully hot, and the powdery smell of the old wood made me sneeze. In the soft mobile light Isabel looked pretty, younger. Her brown hair was laced and tangled in a coiffure which rose over her brow almost as high again as the length of her little face, and resembled an elaborate hat. There was so much of it that I wondered whether she had not pinned on a braid of her shorn-off hair, an unnerving thing which I am told women sometimes do. She had clearly taken a lot of trouble: why, for whom? To cheer herself up, presumably. Poor little Isabel: and I recalled Otto's saying that she was brave.

She was wearing an apricot-coloured linen dress which she explained had just been made for her by Maggie and was not quite complete. The tacking threads were still in it. She was trying it on really. Did I not think it was a pretty colour? Was it quite the right length? With a little air of coy preoccupation she climbed on a stool to survey herself in the big mirror over the fire. Was it not a charming style? I saw her face, a trifle flushed by the heat, reflected in the mirror in intermittent blazes of light as she rotated upon the stool, a golden impression of a plump little midinette. I answered her absently.

"Coffee, Edmund?" She had descended now and was pulling my sleeve. "Do sit down. Must you hurl the cushions out of the chair like that? You are as bad as Otto. Now, what is it, Edmund? Tell me *all* about it."

In asking her to see me I had been unable to be casual, I had scarcely avoided being portentous. I was annoyed with myself and a bit annoyed at Isabel's air of teasing irony, of not taking me quite seriously. I felt for a second some sympathy with Otto's view that irony ought to be a ground for divorce.

I said, in order to find something plausible to say, "I suppose Lydia's will hasn't turned up?"

"No, it hasn't," said Isabel, looking worried. "I've

now looked absolutely everywhere. I think after all she can't have made one. So you boys can have half each. Lydia had plenty of money, you know, though she was so stingy."

Then I said hesitantly, "Isabel, I had a sort of talk with Otto this afternoon—"

"About what you saw last night at the summer-house."

"Oh—well—yes—I—"

"Don't worry," said Isabel calmly. "I know all about it. Only a man as stupid as Otto would have doubted it."

"But how did you know I—"

"I saw you rushing off in pursuit of the lady. One can't have moaning girls on the front lawn without knowing something's amiss. Really, Otto's pathetic if he really imagines it's all a dark secret!"

"I think Otto will be rather relieved to be certain that you know. He doesn't enjoy deception." I chose the words carefully.

"He hasn't the least objection to deception. He just doesn't like the process of being found out. It's bad for his nerves."

"You must think more kindly of him," I said. "He is in great pain about the whole thing and about you."

"Let him suffer, then. But has he really sent you as an emissary? Whatever are you supposed to achieve?" She gave a deliberate gay laugh like releasing a little bird.

[97]

"I'm sorry," I said. "I'm being clumsy. But I am fond of Otto. Ever since I was a child—"

"Well, if you want to talk about *yourself*," she said, "of course that's another matter. I'm quite ready to do that. It would be much more interesting. Let's discuss you, then, Edmund. Now tell me all about your childhood."

I met this as a taunt rather than as a real invitation. Isabel certainly wanted to talk about Otto. Perhaps she was right to castigate my instinctive intrusion of myself.

"Sorry. I'm not the point. I think Otto just wants to feel that we can all be rational about the situation, the fix he's in. He wants to feel it could be talked about, maybe, thought about anyway, without anyone getting into a frenzy. He wants to be able to see where he is. And I do think he really wants to get out."

"He doesn't want to get out," said Isabel. "He wants to be made more comfortable staying in. He wants to feel you've somehow placated me so that he can stop feeling guilty. As for anyone getting into a frenzy, who's likely to, except him? He provides all the frenzies in this house. And what do you mean '*we* can be rational about the situation,' who's we? You were the man who could hardly spare us half an hour of his time. Why didn't you go away like you said you would?"

"After last night—" I mumbled. I hoped she would not mention Flora. I am a very incompetent liar.

"Yes, last night must have been fascinating. Did they put on a show for you?"

I felt I must stop Isabel from speaking in that tone. Her pretty face had put on a jeering expression which I did not like at all. I had certainly blundered into the subject and I did not want merely to upset her. I had been stupid not to realize that Otto had set me an impossible task and one not unjustly characterized by Isabel: he wanted me somehow to "make it all right."

I thought I would try being factual.

"How long have you known, in fact?"

"About Otto and that wretched girl? Oh ages, since the start. They make so much noise, for one thing."

"Noise?"

"Yes, racket, din. Not that I mind what people do. I read in the paper about a man who couldn't make love to his wife unless he had her all tied up in brown paper like a parcel. Otto's classical by comparison. But they do romp about. *C'est un vrai bordel là-bas.*"

I preferred not to go into this. "Isabel, you must really try to be charitable. That poor child—"

"Edmund, don't exasperate me to death!" said Isabel. "And get your big feet out of the way, I want to move the coffee table. I don't *care* about Otto having an affair. I'd be delighted. But I wish he'd have a decent sensible affair with an ordinary girl instead of with a poor slut like that, a sort of demented little tragedy queen. And he treats her like a little animal, the dog that Lydia would never let him have. I've heard them whining and barking at each other! And all more or less underneath my window. It's so petty and disgusting, I hate the muddle of it, the lack of sense—"

"I think Otto could only have an affair with a girl like that," I said, seeing it quite clearly for the first time.

"Then he should live chastely like the rest of us. You know he didn't have any relations with those boys."

"What boys?"

"The apprentices."

"I should hope not!" The possibility had never entered my head.

"You're a naïve creature, Edmund. Just because you've no use for sex you think everyone else is monks and nuns."

This hurt me. How did Isabel know I had no use for sex? It wasn't true anyway.

"That's as may be," I said rather sternly. "As you pointed out, I'm not the subject at issue. May I help you with the wood?"

Isabel was tugging a rather large log out of the box. Together we settled it down on top of the blaze while a cascade of ash between the bars scattered the stone hearth with glowing pebbles. "You ought to have a fireguard, Isabel."

"So Lydia always said. And I didn't point out anything of the sort. I'd much rather talk about you than about Otto." We were now standing face to face at the fire. I shifted slightly, scorched by the fierce glow. I could feel my face as hot and golden as Isabel's. "Shall I show you something, Edmund? Look here."

She held out her hand. I could not at first make out what she was trying to show me. Then I realized it was the hand itself, the hand with the long scar upon it.

"That's where you burnt yourself—"

"*No*," she said with scorn. "Anyone can see that's not a burn! Take it, feel it." She thrust the hand at me as if it were an alien object and I took it gingerly, lightly. It was a little hand. With a slight shiver I felt the smooth depression of the scar.

"What, then—"

Isabel's fingers closed on mine. "Otto did that one day with a chisel. I'll bear the mark till I'm dead. And my God it wasn't the only time—"

"I'm sorry," I said. I was utterly appalled that Otto could have laid hands upon his wife. I knew of course that he was a violent angry man. But I had not imagined this. I am a man of some temper myself at times, but I could not have struck a woman, the very idea sickened me.

"Oh, you know nothing, Edmund, nothing," said Isabel more flatly, turning away. "But you must just try to understand, when you come along so kindly telling me to be charitable, that I've just about had Otto. I don't care how many girls he has."

I stared at my boots. I felt stupid, guilty, sick, and with a physical disgust against both Otto and Isabel which was unfair but overwhelming. I had often been near to thinking of married people as obscene animals, and this vista of this marriage filled me suddenly with a general revulsion. I wanted to get out of the room.

Isabel must have apprehended my feeling, or else perhaps she felt sick too, with Otto, with herself, with it all. She said in a bleak, miserable voice, "You'd better go, Edmund. You've done what Otto told you to do." She tapped a small high-heeled shoe among the embers, which were now a dull red.

I felt dreadfully sorry for her and angry with myself. I wished I could wrench our talk back to some sort of healing simplicity. I said, "Please, Isabel, can't I help you, can't I do *anything?*"

"Of course not. Oh well, yes you can, what task can I set you now? You can remove all the tacking threads from the hem of this dress, that might be within your capacities." She laughed a crazy little laugh. "Here, take these scissors. See you cut off *all* the threads and *don't* cut the material."

She pushed the chairs back to make a space before the hearth. Feeling an idiot, I knelt down awkwardly and began snipping and pulling at the white threads at the hem of the dress. The task began to upset me extremely. I saw at close quarters Isabel's plump nylon-stockinged legs and the white serrated tip of her petticoat. It was difficult not to see more. There was a warm human perfumy smell of soap and scent and clean velvety skin. I tried to keep my hands steady.

"That will do," said Isabel from above.

I put the scissors down on the floor and got up. As I rose I realized at once that something odd had happened. Isabel, like a nymph in a legend, was metamorphosed, changed. Then I saw that she had undone the linen dress all the way down to the waist and was displaying to me two pink round bare breasts.

She stood quite still, looking up at me with a sort of dazed ferocious expression, with vague yearning eyes, her mouth drooping open. I looked at her breasts. It was years since I had seen a woman's breasts. Then I took the linen stuff, which she was holding wide apart, and drew it gently and firmly together again. I felt her little hands fluttering inside mine.

At that moment, or perhaps a second before it, there was a disturbance at the door, a knock, and the sound of someone entering. Both Isabel and I were slowed and confused by the shock of our encounter. Indeed Isabel hardly moved, hardly turned, as Maggie came into the room, carrying a tray, and stopped abruptly in front of our little tableau.

There was a moment's silence and then the door closed again sharply. Isabel and I continued to stare at each other. She began to cry quietly.

TWO

10 ❧ Uncle Edmund
"in Loco Parentis"

The best way of curing a crack in boxwood is to leave the block in a cool damp place for twenty-four hours or so; usually the patient makes a miraculous recovery from quite a severe split. I examined with satisfaction the blocks which I had just retrieved from the cellar. They had healed well. Those who do not work with such material, such thingy, aspects of nature may not quite imagine or credit the way in which a piece of unformed stuff can seem pregnant, inspiring. I can imagine how a sculptor might feel about a lump of stone, though I have never felt this myself. But pieces of wood can quite send my imagination racing even in the handling of them. There is the lovely difference between boxwood and pear wood, the male and the female of the wood-engraver's world. But there is also the strong individual difference between one piece of boxwood and another. Each one is full of a different picture.

It was four days later. I was still waiting, still hanging about. I had no new conception of my role or indeed any clear conception of it at all. And nothing had happened, I had done nothing, Flora had not returned, I could not find her. I was fairly miserable. At moments I told myself that I simply felt "involved" or that I was waiting with morbid curiosity for some outrage of which I could be a useless and somehow gratified spectator. Then I told myself I ought to go. There was a sort of vanity involved in staying, a vain desire to retrieve a lost dignity. I had been more affected than I had liked to admit by Isabel's picture of me as a healer. Having healed no one and failed grossly in the one task where I had a little power of good, I had better, I argued, go home and digest the bitter incompleteness of my excursion. I had better go home and mourn for Lydia.

Yet I stayed. After so much it seemed impossible to go without more. I *was* involved, and in no bad sense. I stayed out of some sort of affection for my brother and sister-in-law, I stayed in order to keep some sort of faith with Flora. I had made more vain telephone calls. I had still not said anything to Isabel. This problem continually tortured me, but I decided it was better to keep quiet. Isabel would be as helpless as I was, and if the worst had happened it might even be better that Isabel should not know at all—or at any rate it seemed fair to leave that decision still in the hands of Flora. I am very literal about promises. And from every point of view Otto was better in the dark. But I was tormented by my responsibility, and by a feeling that I was only keeping quiet because I did not want to resign a sort of privileged position, I did not want the situation to collapse into the hands of Isabel, so that I should become superfluous. I debated the matter continually.

I also tried to think about Lydia, but I could think of no way of thinking about her. It seemed proper to begin now, and here, where there was a sharper sense of her presence, her absence, to weave as it were, to put on, the idea of her death. But I kept seeming to forget that she had died, as if *that* didn't matter, and kept returning in fantasy to the old undying Lydia that I carried inside me. I could not by this sort of meditation invent any decent motive for remaining. And I occasionally thought that I was really only staying on because I could not face the return to my lonely little flat, which became, when I was away from it, quite cold and impersonal as if it forgot me completely as soon as I closed the door. By comparison the rectory was as full of warmth and humours as a pigsty. It was, for all its miseries, a wonderfully inhabited house. And emanating from somewhere within it, I was not sure from where, was a gentle compelling air which made me feel unexpectedly at home.

I had promised Otto that I would help him to go through all Lydia's things, but we kept putting it off. We were still frightened of her, it still seemed a kind of sacrilege to touch her belongings. We halfheartedly sorted out the contents of her desk, which had already been ransacked and disordered by Isabel. There was still no sign of the will, and we concluded there was none. But we found a lot of other things, including all the letters which Otto and I had written her from school, tied up in ribbons, Otto's in a blue ribbon, mine in a pink. We carried these packages unopened down to the kitchen range and burned them. We could not bring ourselves to touch her clothes. There were wardrobes full of the gay long-skirted dresses; and since Isabel refused to have anything to do with the matter we eventually asked Maggie to deal with them. They all then vanished overnight, distributed no doubt to those in the town whom Otto called Maggie's "suppliants."

I had had, after the curious scene in her bedroom, no further "explanation" with Isabel. But some kind of peace or truce existed between us to which I contributed the rather stuffy dignity with which I had managed to carry that occasion off, and Isabel contributed a sort of rueful philosophical contrition. She did better than I did, and I would have liked to make some more definite, more friendly, gesture to her, but I was afraid of initiating some further muddle. In fact the situation was saved by a wordless affection on both sides, and we continued as if nothing had happened, or almost. I did feel I had gained, for better or worse, a clearer vision of Isabel's picture of herself as a sort of sexual queen and empress *manquée*. If she had been a happier woman she would have cast herself as the Lou Andreas-Salomé of her little town. As it was she simply radiated these obscure frenzied little waves of sexual need and would-be authority which, although I was strictly indifferent to them, did have a generally disturbing effect.

I had had no further talk of an intimate kind with Otto and had indeed scarcely seen him, as he seemed now to spend most of the day at the summerhouse. I visited the empty workshop at intervals and was grieved to see his tools so idle. Levkin I saw only in the garden in the distance. Whenever he saw me he would seem to be convulsed with laughter, would gesticulate wildly and then leap into the air. I ignored him.

I had been eating an orange and the dark wood now smelled pungently of the fruit. It was a childhood smell, lingering with a certain combination of the innocent and the disgusting. Oranges are one of the few fruits whose taste I like but whose smell I dislike. I piled the boxwood blocks up neatly and tidied the orange peel on the table. I was sitting in the kitchen. Since yesterday I had discovered that the kitchen suited me rather well. The weather had turned to wind and rain and I was glad of a warm corner. I equally shunned company and the quaint austerity of my father's room, but sitting in the kitchen required no justification. It was a high square place with a shiny linoleum in big black and white checks like a Tintoretto floor. The original Victorian range, a great black machine much cherished by my father, glowed and purred at one end in a large shrine of Dutch tiles, surrounded by dead-beat wicker chairs. The huge deal table, its surface strained and pitted by relentless scrubbing, was as familiar to my hand as to my eye. It had been the natural place to do one's homework, fix one's Meccano, or sort out the inward parts of an electrical device. Here too I had eagerly ruined my first precious blocks of wood. Here I had frequented in sorrow and in joy under the regimes of Carlottas and Giulias and Vittorias as far back as I could remember.

It was about five o'clock in the evening, a time which always finds me fretful and restless. I had a permanent pain of worry about Flora. And I had not yet recovered from the shock which Isabel had given me, a shock now oddly separated from Isabel herself as if a demon had emanated from her which teased me still. I stretched my legs out and contemplated at the other end of the table a heap of cherry-red silk which Maggie had been sewing, presumably a dress for Isabel. Like a true house serf the Italian girl had always made clothes for Isabel and Lydia. Lydia's old beautiful gipsy robes, the garments which my dear father had inspired and which he so much loved to see her wear, had all been made by Maggie: or perhaps by Giulia or Vittoria or Gemma or Carlotta.

Maggie had left her sewing and was busy at a side table with a dismembered chicken and some vegetables. Now the chicken was sizzling softly in a pan while with quick small fingers Maggie plucked the soiled tattered skins from big mushrooms revealing the creamy fleshy discs within. Then on an oval chopping board with brisk little movements she chopped yellowish-white fluted stalks of celery and a large moist onion. The sharp smell of it pricked my eyes, while now Maggie was plucking at a greyish-silver papery integument of garlic and peeling the plump yellow clove within. A glass of red wine stood by her on the table. I looked up from her hands. Her pale bony face had a rather damp, denuded look and her large dark severe eyes were a little dewy from the onion. A strong arabesque at the nostril was echoed in the curve of the long thin mouth. It was a fierce, intelligent yet unprotected face. Her copious hair, pulled harshly back, fell in the long looped bun, black as onyx, shiny as lacquer. She wore no make-up. Had the others looked like that? I could not remember what the others had looked like.

"*Che cosa stai combinando, Maggie?*"

"*Pollo alla cacciatora.*"

There was a sudden loud flurry in the hall outside

and then the sound of someone noisily running up the stairs. I turned sharply and caught a quick snapshot of Flora in hat and coat. I leaped up and was out of the kitchen in a second.

The door of Flora's room banged abruptly in my face, and I heard the key turn in the lock. I pressed the door and said softly, "Flora, Flora—" I scratched on the door like a dog. I did not want to disturb Isabel. I frantically, desperately wanted to see the child alone, to find out what had happened, simply to see her. I was already panting with distress and anxiety. "Please, Flora—"

After a moment or two the door opened quietly and I slipped in. Flora had thrown off her coat and hat. Her hair was piled up in a woven mass behind her head with a lot of clips and pins and she looked older, handsomer. Yet it was still the same transparent, milky, unmarked face of a young girl. She stood very self-consciously straight and upright, her head thrown back defiantly.

"Well, Uncle Edmund, what can I do for you?"

I was almost breathless with shock, with sudden fear and remorse, with some other emotion, on seeing her there so tall, so good-looking, so complete, so full of the unnerving authority of her youth. "Oh Flora, I was so worried about you. I'm so sorry I didn't come that morning. I came later but you'd gone—"

"It doesn't matter," she said. "It wouldn't have made

any difference." She stared at me with a sort of mad radiance in her face.

"What's happened, Flora?"

"I've had it out!" She laughed shortly.

"Oh God." I sat down on her bed. I had known it, of course I had known it at once, when she had gone, that this was how it would be. But I felt a new pain, I felt like a murderer. "You shouldn't have—"

"I decided all your moral stuff was no good. There are moments when one's got to follow one's instincts, when one's got to do what one wants. And I wanted to tear that thing right out of me. If I'd had that child I would have killed it."

"You have killed it." The words were brutal, but it was myself I was accusing.

"It isn't like that!" She stamped her foot. "What do you know about it? You're a man. You can't imagine what it's like to feel that cancer inside you, to feel it eating up your youth, your happiness, your freedom, your whole future. Men can moralize! But whoever heard about the problems of unmarried fathers? They haven't any problems!"

I knew it would be useless and unkind to reproach her now. She was filled to the brim with that sense of her right to freedom, her right to happiness, which makes the young, when they confront their elders, so unattractive and so ruthless. No man has a right to happiness or the right, for that, to trample upon other lives. Yet turning, with an old automatic movement, all the rebuke upon myself, I thought: I can see this so clearly because I have long ago given up my own hopes of being happy. She has still a happy destiny.

We were facing each other, I still seated and she leaning against the edge of the window, her chin lifted, her hands nervously smoothing her smart tartan pinafore dress. She looked very pretty and full of the new life which that surrendered life had given her. I felt a pang of resentful envy and felt at the same time a sort of admiration for her sheer vitality.

Disturbed, routed by her, I said, "I hope at least you were sensible and had the thing done well—"

"Oh, the very best! Someone lent me some money."

"Mr. Hopgood, I suppose. And how does *he* feel about it?" I could hear the tones of age and envy in my voice but I could not check them. I could almost have put my head in my hands and wept with rage and sadness at it all. And the thing that mattered most, that she had consented to end a human life, was already being swept from me, tiny and lost as the embryo itself.

"Hopgood?" She looked at me for a moment without understanding. Then she began to laugh wildly. "Oh, Charlie Hopgood, bless him! He was a complete fiction. I just invented a name on the spur of the moment."

"You mean—it was someone else?"

"How quick you are, Uncle Edmund! Yes, it was someone else, and just guess who!"

I rose to my feet and she sat down and crossed her legs, adjusting her skirt at the knee. I could see now that she was shivering with emotion.

I groped. "I don't know, Flora—"

"Look about the house, look about you. There's a pretty boy, a pretty little billygoat—"

"My God. Levkin. Surely not. You don't mean David Levkin—he was the father—?"

"Oh, how *stupid* you are! Yes, of course. Wasn't it obvious? Why can't you guess and understand? And why do you have to say everything out in that crude way? You're so brutal to me. Men are all so brutal and beastly. Look at my father. He's just like a great monster, a rhinoceros or something, ugly, violent, horrible. And you're just the same. . . ." Her voice was high and tearful. She put her hands to her face, one covering her mouth, the other with fingers spread on her brow as if to stop her head from bursting open.

I looked down at her strained, pressing fingers. I felt for a moment almost faint with rage. David Levkin. "Why didn't you tell me?"

She whipped her hands away. Her face was red and wet and she almost bared her teeth at me. "Why should I? Have you any right to the truth? You never come here, I hardly know you. I told you because I had to tell somebody, and much good you were! But I wasn't sure you wouldn't tell Father, with all your namby-pamby ideas. And I didn't want Father to break David's neck."

"Why are you telling me now?" I spoke coolly, but I was all a confused fire within. I could well understand her fears about Otto.

"Oh, it somehow doesn't matter now. Now I'm all right—"

"Well, don't worry, I won't tell."

"I don't care what you do, Uncle Edmund. You're of no further interest to me. Oh, you don't like it, do you, I can see you don't like it! But you can take yourself away now. There's nothing more to stay for. The show's over. You've been living in a monastery, haven't you? Now your head's turned because you've seen some real women. Well, go back to it, go back to your crippled life. Leave real living to people who are able for it."

She got up and turned her back on me and began to powder her face, peering into the little heart-shaped mirror on her dressing table. Her full tartan skirt swung up impertinently like a bell as she leaned forward.

I stood there like an ape with my hands hanging. I could not leave her like this. Her words hurt exceedingly. But I felt rather as if I had to beg her pardon for having made her utter such ugliness. "Flora, I quite realize—"

"Oh, don't be such a *bore*," she said in a tired voice,

busy with lipstick. "No one wants you here. Go home
and play with your little bits of wood."

I stared at the white sleeves of the blouse which she
was wearing under the white pinafore dress. The
sleeves were pushed up to the elbow, revealing her
forearms, round and biscuit-coloured. I saw this with
the clarity of a beloved detail in a picture, it seemed to
detach itself in my mind from the appalling medley of
anger and self-abasement. Hardly knowing what I did,
I stepped forward and took hold of her arm. "Flora—"

I must have gripped her harder than I intended, for
she winced and gave a little cry, jerking away from me.
She moved her other hand as if to strike me, or perhaps
just to push me away, and I caught it in flight like a
bird and crumpled it in my palm. "Flora, please—"
I wanted simply to make her still, to console her,
to stop her from speaking to me so harshly, to ease the
pain that made her do so. But now something quite else
seemed to be happening. As I saw her furious face
close to mine, saw her tongue and her teeth, she kicked
me painfully in the shin. I released her hand and slid
my arm round her waist and drew her so tightly up
against me that she could no longer struggle. As I felt
her become limp in my arms I lowered my face with a
groan into her hair, which was becoming undone and
falling down onto my sleeve. I stared at the long
strands of golden-red hair on my dark sleeve. It was
another detail.

There was a sound behind me. As I let Flora go,

setting her as it were gently upon her feet, I was aware
without turning my head that David Levkin was
standing in the doorway. Then there was a furious
dishevelled flurry, and like a wild cat escaping from a
room Flora had darted past Levkin out of the door.
Levkin closed the door behind her and stood looking
at me. I sat down on the bed and covered my face
with my hands.

11 ❧ *A Modern Ballet*

Now with one hand I controlled my heart, which was striking my side like a desperate animal. With the other I smoothed back my hair and rubbed my face over. I felt as if my face must have altered, must have become distorted with chagrin and shame. For a moment I was hardly aware of Levkin.

When my breathing was calmer and I had rubbed my face into some sort of order I looked up at him. He was in the same attitude by the door, one hand on the door handle, the other holding up his white unbuttoned shirt at the neck. The broad full lips were soft and amused, but the eyes had almost vanished in wrinkles of sardonic wariness.

At last he said, "Well, Uncle Edmund, how is it with you?"

I stared at him in silence and he moved a little nervously away from the door, placing a chair between myself and him. "Well, Uncle, what price Sir Galahad now, what price Saint Edmund the Confessor?"

"So it was you," I said.

"It was me. Lucky, lucky me."

"Otto trusted you." I spoke softly. I was aware now of the blessed rage within me, a sacred rage purging my shame. "He trusted you, and—"

"Lord Otto is deaf and blind. He has other fish to fry. As for you, why should I submit to you? Why should I not draw your blood a little? You were so beautifully caught, Uncle Edmund, were you not? But no—*you* shall reproach *me*. Speak daggers, daggers, I deserve it!" He laughed and with a dramatic gesture threw wide his shirt, which was unbuttoned to the waist. Then he moved, swinging the chair with him, as I rose to my feet.

"You don't seem to know what you've done—" I choked over the words. I wanted to cover him with leeches and scorpions, I wanted to make him cringe and whimper.

He skipped before me like a bland, gay child. "Oh, but I do, I do! What does it say in the Gospels? 'Whoso shall offend one of these little ones, it were better for him that a millstone were hanged about his neck and that he were drowned in the depth of the sea.' I am that man, I am that man!" He gabbled the quotation delightedly. "But what else does it say in the Gospels, dear Uncle? 'Let him who is without sin among you cast the first stone.' " He danced gleefully behind his chair, edging a little towards the window.

"You must leave this house," I said. This at least was something I could impose upon him. "I can't think how you can have the impertinence to remain here after—"

"Uncle, Uncle, no coarse language—remember, we are in a lady's boudoir!" He dodged back again towards the door, still interposing the chair between us. As he moved he picked up something white from the bed, flourished it in front of me, and then half buried his face in it, peering at me over the top. I saw that what he held was Flora's white flimsy nightdress. I began to tremble.

"Fair flowers and ripe berries, dear Uncle. We like them both, don't we, we enjoy them both. And when we fall we know where we like to fall. Why, even you —or do I wrong you, Uncle dear? Perhaps you don't really like girls? Perhaps you prefer boys, delicious milk-white boys as beautiful as angels? But no—you don't really like anything at all, Uncle, not anything at all. And that is why you hate us, you hate to see us at it. Isn't that it, Uncle Edmund?" He spoke softly, peering at me now through a fringe of brown hair, his body immobile and taut, ready to leap.

I didn't raise my voice. "Go away, Levkin, or I shall

probably hit you." I was beginning to be frightened of the anger.

He half turned the door handle behind him, but he seemed delighted, fascinated by his power to enrage me. "Hit me, then, beat me! If a man strike you on one cheek, offer him the other. I offer you both cheeks, Uncle. I offer you— Ah!"

I moved slightly and he half opened the door, ready to dart out. His face was bland, broad, flattened with smiling mockery; his eyes were two gleaming exultant arcs. The nostrils arched with happy impertinence.

He went on softly, "And yet why should I consent to be chastised by you? Old rhino, old rhino! Oh yes, I was listening to it all at the door! I only came in because I could not see enough through the keyhole. And you were worth seeing, Nuncle, you were! Here, take this. You might enjoy this, pawing it over in your stable!" He threw the nightdress into my face.

I slapped the lacy stuff to the ground with one hand and reached for him with the other. My fingers touched his shirt as he eluded me, flying past and springing lightly onto the bed. He lifted the chair, pointing the legs towards me.

"Ah, not here, not here," he said softly. His dishevelled shirt had partly emerged from his trousers, and he was panting with excitement. "Not in Flora's pretty room with all her little things. This is no place to play at rhinos. Outside, if you will. But make no mistake. I can wrestle and I would defend myself. Perhaps it would be delightful. But no, no. The one who will kill me will be Otto. And when that time comes I shall not resist him."

I took one of the legs of the chair and pulled it away from him. Fortunately he let it go easily and then stood before me on the bed, slowly spreading his arms in an attitude of defenceless submission. The hot moment passed.

I felt incoherent, disgusted, wretched, I loathed him, I loathed myself. I wanted to end the scene cleanly somehow. I said, "I won't tell Otto, but you must clear out."

"I will go when I am ready," he said. "My sister is well here. And do you want to drive Lord Otto insane? Oh Edmund, Edmund, how I enjoy you! You are a buffoon just like your brother but you don't even know it! He, at least, he knows that he is a perfectly ludicrous animal."

"I won't tell Otto," I said, "but I will tell Isabel. And now—"

He laughed outrageously. "Oh, Isabel! She! No, no, it is too beautiful. No, she will tell *you* things, poor rhino, poor ox, she will goad you, she will drive you in harness! But I was forgetting, you are the Health Visitor, the General Inspector! Well, you shall know, you shall know. Yes, come and see Isabel. She will tell and tell."

He gave a great leap from the bed and as he went by he tapped me lightly on the chest. I subsided abruptly into a chair. I could hear him now on the landing, calling, "Isabel! Isabel!"

12 ❧ Isabel Confesses

Isabel locked the door behind me and turned the gramophone down a little. "What was David shouting about?" She looked plump and dishevelled in a shabby blue silk dressing gown with the sleeves rolled up. She looked crumpled, sleepy, vague, a bit frightened. Perhaps she had been lying down. "What is it, Edmund? You look rather mad too." She stared at me. Intimations of Wagner rumbled in the background.

"Flora's back," I said. I looked down at Isabel and felt myself indeed clownlike and gaping.

"I know. Whatever has David been doing to you, Edmund? He pushed you in through the door like a dog! No, you sit down, I'll stand. I can't sit still these days, I'm too nervous."

I sat down on a fat embroidered stool which yelped under me. The high bright coronet of the wood fire subsided, bringing a musty fragrance and such a blaze of warmth in my back that I had to edge away. The room flickered with golden light. Isabel wandered among the furniture like a distraught nymph waist-deep in the reeds. She caressed her two forearms vigorously. The blue dressing gown caught at surfaces and edges and she plucked it away with jerks of the knee.

"Isabel, do you know about Flora?"

"So you feel it your duty to tell me?"

"So you know?"

"That Flora was pregnant? Oh yes, yes."

"And did you, do you, know who it was that made her so?"

"Yes. David Levkin. He's probably listening at the door at this moment." She moved across and picked up a log of wood. The dry powdery bark dusted her sleeve and floated in the air.

"But Isabel, you tolerated him in the house—" I sneezed violently. The bark was like pepper.

"How Victorian you are, Edmund. How could I turn him out? Besides, the damage was done. Put that on the fire, would you."

"I can perfectly understand," I said, "that you should not have told Otto. Otto might go berserk. But oughtn't you to have told Levkin to go? After all—"

"Oh, do stop telling us what we ought to do. And

do stop sneezing. It annoys me so much when people sneeze."

"Sorry, I've got a rather sensitive nose—"

"Damn your nose. I know I rather encouraged you. You gave me a moment of hope. But it's too much of a tangle, really. Don't ask any more, Edmund. It's better not to know."

She kicked her way to the mantelpiece and surveyed herself in the mirror, absently tapping her wedding ring against the marble. Then she picked up a jar of cold cream and began to smooth it into the skin under her eyes with little patting movements.

"I've seen too much already," I said. "I can't shut my eyes now. You realize that Flora has got rid of the child?"

Isabel moved impatiently and her gown brushed my knees. I got up hastily, trampled on the stool, and retreated to the other side of the rug.

"You've broken it. Oh, you are a beastly clumsy animal. There's no need to jump like that when I come near you. And how can you talk so crudely about Flora—"

I felt agitated, exasperated, confused. Somehow it was all too scandalous, too outrageous. Levkin must be made to go, Flora must be made to realize what she had done, Isabel must be made to take some responsibility for the whole scene. "I'm sorry," I said. "I find it all pretty shocking and surprising. And you seem to be taking it so calmly."

"Calmly!" She gave a deliberate grimace of pain which transformed her face into a violent mask. She moved to the gramophone, turned it up for a moment to a deafening roar, and then lowered it till there was nothing but a distant beat. "Calmly!" she said more softly with her back to me. "One is not calm on the rack. One is not calm in the fire. Oh, you are stupid. And I looked forward to you so much."

"Isabel, I'm sorry," I said. "I can't heal you, I'm not good enough. I'm in a muddle myself. I just feel there's something here I don't understand. Could you explain it to me, please?" I was certainly following Levkin's instructions to the letter.

"Yes, me. You don't understand me. And neither do I." She fell on her knees in front of the fire, closing her eyes against the great heat. "I'm the missing link."

I stared down at her. Her dark hair was unkempt, wispy, straying bleakly upon her neck. "How did you find out about Flora, anyway?" I asked her.

"David told me."

"What perfect effrontery! If Levkin—"

"Do stop calling him Levkin. He's practically one of the family. Oh, can't you see, can't you see? I feel it must be written on the walls of this room, written on my face, on my hands—"

"What?"

"I love him, I love him, I love him—"

"You mean—?"

"David, yes, David. I love him, I'm crazy with love,

overwhelmed, absolutely done for—oh God!" She suddenly rolled over on the floor at my feet and took a firm grip of one of my ankles.

I stood paralysed and speechless with shock and suddenly nauseated as if some overpowering smell had entered the room. Levkin here too, Levkin everywhere. I was utterly surprised and shocked at Isabel's words, and her whole being was for a moment repugnant. I began to mumble and pull myself away.

"Yes, I love him." She let go, still lying there limp, face downward on the ground, her silky legs revealed. "I worship him. I want him, I want his child. I even wanted that child of Flora's, the child she killed. If I could have had even Flora's child to keep—" Her voice became thick and trembling.

I kicked the disabled stool aside and sat down heavily in a chair. I could not forget that Isabel had made an appeal to me, an appeal which had touched me to the heart, although I had rejected it. Now I saw her for an instant as she lay on the floor as an abandoned woman, a harlot. I wanted to shake her, to interrogate her. "I suppose Otto doesn't know *this?*"

"No, of course not. I am still alive." Her voice came muffled through her hair.

"How long—?"

"Ever since he came. I fell in love with him the moment I saw him in Otto's workshop, or it might have been the next moment. It was like a lightning flash and everything becoming golden, like the end of the world. Oh, you can't conceive what a lonely idiotic life I've led. I've seen no one for years except that monster Otto and those dreadful boys. I know it's my own fault. I somehow wanted it all to be miserable and dreary so as to punish Otto and Lydia. But then when David came, it was a vision of life, it was like seeing an angel, it was like seeing a god. Can't you see even now how beautiful he is? Can't you at all imagine being in love with him?"

"Yes," I said, "oddly enough I can. But when you found he had—seduced Flora, surely—"

Isabel sat up and adjusted her gown over her knees. Her face was calmer and rather dreamily deliberate. She patted a log back into the fire. "I had him first, you see," she said softly.

"But—"

"He only took up with Flora because I tried to break with him. He did it to spite me."

"He—then—loved you?"

"I don't know. He wanted me. He found he could have me."

"You mean you actually—"

"Oh yes, Edmund, everything. Everything, everything, everything. And if we could have thought of more we would have done that too. Otto with the sister and I with the brother. Oh, it worked wonderfully!" She turned to look at me now with a dreadful bold calm. Her face shone with a resigned, broken beauty.

"Oh, Isabel—"

"You're scandalized."

I was scandalized, horrified. I was also, I had just realized, and the realization was sobering, jealous. I felt excluded. Yet surely I did not want to be inside such a circle of hell? "But you tried to break it off?"

"Well, yes. Lydia was dying in the house, practically in the next room. I think I felt rather as Otto did. We both tried about the same time to break the— addiction. I felt sick with myself. Lydia suffering so dreadfully, and all that at the same time. It was rotten. And of course I was scared absolutely stiff of Otto finding out. I am scared absolutely stiff."

"He's got no notion?"

"No. He can think of nothing but Elsa. It's the first real relation he's had with a woman in years, perhaps ever. It was never much good with me. They were both, for both of us, a godsend."

I hated hearing her talk like this. "But Isabel—honestly I am rather scandalized. These are—purely physical relationships—"

"Oh Edmund, Edmund, Edmund," she said wearily. She rose slowly, laboriously, like a stout elderly person. I rose too.

"But what are you going to do now?" I asked her.

"I don't know. Just go blindly on. We are both in the pockets of those changelings."

"You mean you would—re-establish relations with that boy, after Flora—" I recalled what Otto had said about the dreaming Eve of Autun, the root of all evil. Isabel simply didn't seem to know what she was doing.

"I don't think you've understood me, Edmund," said Isabel. "I am in love. I agree that this is a form of madness, but at least it's a fairly well-known form. Or perhaps you don't know about it? 'An arrow in the side makes poor travelling, only not to run is a worse pain.'"

"You are raving," I said. "Otto could so easily find out, and—"

"I know. I feel like a ship moving steadily towards an iceberg. But I can no other. Don't you see I'm *in extremis*? The only question is, when Otto finds out, will he kill David or me or both?"

She looked so pale and small, her arms hanging limply by her sides, as if she were already pinned helplessly to a wall. I felt suddenly sorry and frightened for her. She looked like a victim. "What can I do for you, Isabel?"

"One thing. Take Flora away."

I half turned from her. The memory of my grapple with Flora came back with photographic clarity. That was the one rational thing which I could have done, protect Flora, and I had systematically and now completely made it impossible.

"Yes, take her away, Edmund. She's fond of you and she trusts you. Take her to your house. Her term isn't starting yet and she simply mustn't stay here.

There'll be some outrage. If she stays here we shall all of us go mad."

As I listened to her tones of entreaty I thought of another thing. Levkin would certainly tell Isabel that he had seen me seizing Flora. I was filled with confused, angry distress. "Can't you help Flora yourself, Isabel?"

"Don't be a fool. She loves him too. Flora will never forgive me between now and the end of her life. David told me he had made her pregnant. He returned to *me*, he came back to me with *that* confidence, with *that* simplicity. How can she ever forgive our having spoken of this together, consulted about her together? Don't you know what the pride of a young girl is like? And the first time, the very first time. Ah, poor, poor child." Tears were coming to Isabel at last, big slow tears such as one can only weep for oneself when one pities oneself in the guise of another.

"I agree Flora would be better out of the house. And then you—"

"And then I can get on with it? Well, that won't be your affair, Edmund. You must leave Otto and me to our merry-go-round. You remember what I said about Saint Teresa's cupboard in hell? You thought I was exaggerating, didn't you?"

"Oh my dear, I will try and help. I'll do what I can. I'm sorry I'm such a fool."

"That's all right, Edmund. You'd better go now. Please look after Flora. And, Edmund—"

"Yes?"

"Do you mind if I kiss you? I'm sorry about the shock tactics last time. I was just a bit mad then because of David. I don't know if you understand."

I didn't quite. "I understand." I took small, plump, tear-stained Isabel in my arms and kissed her hot eyes and her brow. Her arms clutched my neck violently for a moment and I let her find my lips. It seemed like a desperate farewell. As I held her then I felt sad and deprived in all my being and felt from top to toe the same sadness in her.

13 ❧ *Edmund Runs to Mother*

"Maggie."

It was very quiet in the kitchen, with a kind of distilled quietness, after the recent hubbub of Isabel. It seemed a place of sanity and recollection.

Now Maggie had been washing Otto's underwear. There was an intimate smell of warm wet wool. Steaming piles of vests and long pants lay in a big blue plastic basket. One by one she took the garments and stretched them into shape and laid them over the slats of a wooden drying-rail which had been lowered from the ceiling by a pulley. I recalled this ritual very well from childhood, the strong, neat movement of the hands as they pulled the garments straight, the hands of Giulia and Carlotta and Vittoria. I sat down to watch, feeling, with a mixture of shyness and familiarity, included in the scene, comfortably included in her consciousness although she had not replied to my exclamation, had scarcely looked in my direction. My half-eaten orange and the pile of boxwood blocks lay still at one end of the table, and at the other were Maggie's sewing, her work box and scissors. I watched her quick, rhythmical movements. The line of Otto's things lengthened.

I looked up at her face and found her looking at me. Her eyes, with that damp strange animal look, seemed forbidding and suspicious. I felt troubled by a sharp need to talk to her, together with a paralysing absence of wit. I felt extremely upset, ill-used, lacerated, I wanted comfort: yet how could I ask for it here? I looked quickly down.

It was a dark, rainy evening and the light in the kitchen was uncertain, as if things were constantly moving and shifting just at the corner of one's vision. The twilight began to trouble me. I felt distressed in all my body and almost frightened. I knew I ought to go upstairs and sit alone and think about what Isabel had said to me, but I could not go away. I moved abruptly and switched the light on. There was a miserable glow, more like fog than like light, scarcely brighter than the damp, sulphurous illumination outside. Maggie, who had jumped slightly at my movement, stared at me and then returned to her task.

I ranged about the kitchen in the dirty muted haze,

touching things here and there. I ached with discomfort and distress. "God, what a rotten light. You couldn't possibly sew by this light. I hope you don't try. Lydia was so mean. Are there any stronger bulbs in the cupboard? Ah yes, a hundred watts, that's better. Could you turn the light out again? All right, I'll take my shoes off."

I mounted the table to fix the new bulb. My hair brushed the ceiling. Maggie was looking up at me in the shifting twilight, her face a blur, her eyes big and black. She stretched out a hand to help me descend. I felt the small hand warm and damp from the washing. It seemed a long way down. Then she moved to the door and a very bright light dazzled us. I covered my eyes. Yes, Lydia was dead.

The garden outside was suddenly a dark blue square, misty and insubstantial, withdrawn. I went to pull the gay red and blue William Morris curtains. The kitchen was enclosed and bright now like a compact little ship, everything in it brimful of radiant colour. I felt a little better. Maggie spread out Otto's pants upon the rail, a wide outrageous forked pennant. I sat on the table and began to destroy the remainder of the orange.

"It's funny, isn't it," I said to her, "you must have been taller than me when we first met."

"No. You were already taller, much taller. You are thinking of Vittoria."

"Where do you come from in Italy, Maggie? I've stupidly forgotten. Verona?"

"No, that was Giulia. I come from Rome."

"Rome, of course. I remember your showing us pictures."

"Have you been to Rome?"

It seemed odd she should not know. And yet why should she? "No. Florence, Venice. Not Rome. You remember you said you'd take us there, kidnap us? We had quite a fantasy about it. Or was that Carlotta?"

"No, that was me. Carlotta came from Milan."

Her voice was that of a cultivated English person with only a very light accent. She had been an educated, intelligent girl. What had condemned her to a wasted life in this sombre household?

"I'm afraid you're all mixed up in my mind," I said. "I wonder where *they* are now—"

"Married." She spoke it as if it were the name of a distant country.

In a sudden flurry of distress I went on hastily, "People in the north dream of the south. I wonder do people in the south dream of the north. Did you?"

"I had a dream of the north once, a dream of strength."

This distressed me too, though I could not say why. I watched her briskly haul the drying-rail up to the roof. Otto's enormous underwear swayed in the warm air from the range, blatantly unmentionable.

Something in the sight of my brother's things displayed in a row like a fatuous grinning army produced a rush of irritation and some more painful emotion. I wanted to sweep Otto right out of the way. Then I knew that I was going to leap the divide and appeal to Maggie for help. I said, "I've been a failure since I arrived here."

Maggie slowly dried her hands on the towel. She looked at me with an expression of faint interest. She seemed aware of the extent of my appeal. But she just said, "And now you are going away?"

Her cool acceptance of my remark hurt me unexpectedly much. It was not that I wanted to be told I was doing well, or that no one could have managed better: but I found I cared what Maggie thought about me.

"Can I help anyone by staying?"

"Possibly not anyone else. Yourself perhaps."

She said it in such a dry way, almost a metaphysical way, I could hardly bear it. I was shamefully in need of sympathy, of warmth. I did not want to be dissected and despoiled.

"I don't think the question of *me* arises," I said rather irritably. "There is nothing for *me* here."

She looked at me with those eyes which always seemed near tears and yet at the same time so cold. "The question of oneself always arises, doesn't it?"

This was painfully true. And of course if I stayed, I confessed it now, I would stay because of some need of my own. I felt that I was fencing with Maggie and getting the worst of it. There was a tension in the air, an obscure sense of direction. I said to her, "I suppose you know more or less what's going on in this house?"

"I think I know altogether what's going on in this house."

"How?"

"People have loud voices. Everyone shouts a great deal here. Perhaps the pipes conduct the sound. I seem to hear everything in the kitchen." She spoke with an extreme catlike softness; it was the voice of the unseen observer, of the eternally silent superior servant.

I imagined Maggie working there alone in the kitchen, peeling the mushrooms and pouring the red wine into the *pollo*, washing Otto's unspeakably filthy pants, and listening to the secret life of the house. It was a weird thought. Then at the next moment it was a disagreeable one. Maggie must have overheard my exchanges with Levkin. We were not exactly whispering. I looked at her uneasily, at her sallow secretive southern face. She had returned to her sewing.

I got up restlessly and began to pace about. My body still felt disturbed and unhappy. The leg of one of Otto's undergarments slapped me damply in the eye and I irritably thrust it off. What was an intelligent girl like Maggie doing wasting her time washing Otto's things for him? The mad idea flashed across my mind that I might ask Maggie to come and be my housekeeper. But that was idiotic. There was no place for a housekeeper in my three miserable rooms. I said suddenly, "I don't want to leave here."

"Don't, then."

She looked up at me, but I avoided her glance. I resented her display of indifference. I could not endure being treated so coldly. I felt I was being deprived of some natural right. I knew I ought now to keep silence, to retrieve dignity, to leave her. But the warm words came tumbling out of my mouth, the old impulse to confession, the final weak appeal for comfort. "I'll have to go, I've made such a mess of things. Particularly with Flora, I've been such a clumsy idiot with Flora. Isabel asked me to look after her, to take her away home with me, but I can't. I don't know how it happened but just now, upstairs, I sort of took hold of her, I frightened her. And after all she's been through, poor wretched child. Of course I meant no harm, but now she won't trust me an inch. Only someone's got to help her, and I do think she should go away. Oh God, Maggie, I am a fool!"

"*Che peccato.* Do you often jump on young girls?"

"I haven't touched a woman in years!" The words fell out between us, and then I blushed scarlet with rage at her asking and at my answering. Nor did it ease me to recall that she had also witnessed and doubtless misunderstood the scene with Isabel. The notion that Maggie might think me a philanderer provoked an incoherent apoplexy of indignation. Yet at the same time I violently regretted having made the admission. Such things were nobody's business but my own.

She seemed to be accepting what I said with cool, credulous interest. "No girls at all? And no boys either?"

"*No!*" I added more quietly, "Certainly not!" and glared into those rather moist dark eyes.

She gave a secretive little smile and returned to her sewing. I found myself hot with emotion. There are things which may be thought but should not be said. I felt a strong resentment against Maggie for her directness, for having so unfairly startled me out of my reticence. I felt too perhaps some primeval male fear of a woman's contempt. Yet I had started this rather confused and unmanageable conversation.

I looked at her now, remote and self-contained as a cat: the cunning little smile, the thin fine line of the mouth and the downy hairs above it, the dark golden yet transparent skin, the sober downcast eyes. She seemed a chaste figure, now more like a priestess than like a nun, a keen, severe little priestess. She reminded me vaguely of something in a painting. Yet I had seen that face before I had seen any painting, perhaps before I had seen any face.

"I think," said Maggie, still attending to her sewing, "that you ought to apologize to Flora. You might be able to win her confidence again. She certainly needs somebody she can trust."

"There aren't any words for that apology. Can't *you* help Flora?"

"I too have lost my power to help. Acts have their

consequences. Your mother set us all at odds. As you can imagine."

I could imagine. "But surely no one could hold anything against *you*. Surely you are perfectly innocuous."

"Because I am so little, almost invisible, like a mouse—"

"No, no, *no*, I mean you are good."

"Like you, yes!"

"Oh, stop it, Maggie," I said. I clashed the boxwood blocks sharply together like castanets.

"Stop what?"

What indeed. I looked down with distressed, exasperated puzzlement at the small familiar large-eyed face.

"Oh, excuse *me*," said Flora from the doorway.

14 ❧ *Otto Selects a Victim*

Flora banged the door behind her with her foot. She looked flushed and untidy. Her hair was a shaggy mass almost toppling forward over her brow, and a bronzy glow surrounded her head where curly tendrils had escaped from the arrangement. Her short upper lip thrust suspiciously forward and her upturned nose wrinkled and quivered. She drew her tartan dress closer to her legs in an unconscious gesture of self-defence, perhaps disgust. But she ignored me and addressed herself to Maggie.

"I've brought the change." She spoke in a deliberately harsh and rasping voice. She advanced to the table and with a theatrical gesture threw onto it a heap of five-pound notes. Then she could not stop herself from glancing at me.

Maggie, who had risen, quietly gathered the notes together and began to count them. As the meaning of the scene dawned on me I felt an immediate shocked repulsion at the sight of the two women with the pile of money between them. It was like a scene in a brothel.

"Yes," said Flora. "I got it cheap because the doctor was such a dear old man and I was such a dear little girl! And Maggie lent me the money because she's a woman, or used to be. But I don't exactly love her for it. You're all a lot of monkeys as far as I'm concerned. I—"

"Flora, please," I said, "just listen to me for a minute. This is important. You must try to forgive me for what happened upstairs. I didn't mean to frighten you like that and I'm very sorry. I don't quite know how it happened. Anyway I apologize and I hope I haven't entirely lost your affection and your confidence. I shall certainly try to deserve them if you'll give me another chance. I think it would be a good thing if you came and stayed at my house for a little while. You need a bit of rest and peace, and I should be very happy if you'd come. Or if I can help you in any other way I should be only too glad. Whether or not you come and stay with me, I do think you would be better away from this house for a while. Don't you think so too?"

Flora stared at me, her flushed face pulled into a self-conscious sneer. "Uncle Edmund, you're pathetic. Did Maggie put you up to it?"

"No, well— But won't you try to forgive me?"

"Don't be silly. I can't arrange what I feel. I just hate the sight of you, that's all. As for your not knowing what came over you, I think you'd better wake up to yourself. I'd see a good psychoanalyst if I were you!"

"I'm sorry you feel like that, Flora. As I say, I do humbly apologize. But, seriously, don't you think you ought to go away from here?"

"So that Mummy can have a clear run with darling David? I suppose *she* put you up to it!"

"No, no. Use your common sense, child. Everything here is in an awful tangle and you're better out of it. Anything could happen."

"You mean when Daddy finds out. Yes, that's what I'm dying to see, what happens when Daddy finds out. You want me to miss all the fun!"

"Don't be a perfect idiot. You've done quite enough harm already. You must realize that. The least you can do is to try to minimize the consequences."

" 'Minimize the consequences'!" She mimicked me. "So you're judging me, are you, the two of you, like a couple of pious parents with their erring little girl! Count it carefully, Maggie, and see I haven't cheated you. As if I would have taken your bloody money if I could have got it anywhere else! I regret nothing I've done and I'm certainly not accountable to *you*. And

I'm not little Alice in Wonderland any more, Uncle Edmund, thanks to people like you, except that you wouldn't have had the guts for it. This is my home and I'm staying in it. Why don't *you* go away? You've only made yourself ridiculous here and no one likes you!"

I was hurt by her words and even more by the new aggressive ugliness of her face as she spoke them. It was a terrible growing up. I groaned for my hopeless lack of the right kind of authority.

"Flora, I'm not judging you. I'm in no position to judge anyone. I know I'm ridiculous. But you are my niece and I want to help—"

"You're just an old goat, Uncle Edmund, why not admit it? Your goody-goody act doesn't take anyone in any more. I expect you're impotent into the bargain. Why don't you go home and look at your obscene photos?"

"Flora," said Maggie quietly, "stop shouting and talk to us sensibly. You know perfectly well you can't stay on here. Your mother will never come to her senses while you are in the house."

Flora advanced on Maggie, and her voice rose to an incoherent whine of fury. "You! You can stop telling me what to do. Just because you lent me that money you think you own me, don't you! But I know all about you, Maggie Magistretti. And if this house is crazy you've certainly done your bit in making it so!"

I could see the child was becoming hysterical and

ought to be slapped or bundled straight out of the door. But I also knew that I could not possibly touch her. I banged on the table. "Flora, go back to your room—"

She turned on me. Her lips were wet and trembling, and tears were spilling from her eyes. "Oh, you don't know about Maggie! Well, I'll tell you. She had a horrible, horrible thing with Lydia. It was beastly and it made the whole house horrible. And just because she doesn't attract men—"

I felt pain, shock, anger, and a horrified impulse to close her mouth. But as she moved, in fact I recoiled. Flora struck the table violently, sweeping the pile of money up into a flurry of notes which flew to every part of the kitchen. Maggie was saying something in Italian and reaching out her hands in a deprecating gesture. I saw Flora's face flushed and distorted and the reddish-golden hair beginning to fall forward over her brow as if her head were coming in two. She seized Maggie by the wrist and jerked her forward, and in a moment the two women merged into a swaying, stumbling intaglio. I backed away from them as if they were scuffling animals. Then I saw that Flora had got hold of Maggie's scissors and was flourishing them like a knife. For a moment I almost expected blood to flow—and then as the two came apart I saw that Flora had sheared through Maggie's hair at the nape of the neck. With an exclamation of horror and disgust Flora dropped the oblong knob of hair onto the table, where it unravelled into a black snake. There was silence.

I sat down on the window seat. I had never seen two women fighting, and the sight of it was utterly nauseating. Flora, her mouth wide open and dribbling, was staring at the limp dead length of hair. She still held the scissors high up like a weapon. Maggie drew her hands slowly about her shorn neck and then covered her face and her breast with the gesture of one suddenly made naked. At that moment Otto came in.

The appearance of Otto filled me with terror even before I knew what was going to happen, and I felt too, for the women, for myself, an immediate crippling sense of guilt. It must have seemed a strange scene: Flora now lifting the severed hair with an almost ritual gesture, Maggie metamorphosed into some quite other being, hiding her face as if from the gaze of Medusa, and the table and floor strewn with five-pound notes.

Otto looked and at once took in the essence of what had happened. He entered like a master, moving straight into action. In two strides he reached Flora. He took the trophy from her. The scissors clattered to the floor. Then he took one of her hands in his and slapped it hard with his other hand. I had often seen him do this when she was a child.

Such a slap from Otto was no light matter. Flora reacted as she had done on the past occasions. Her face became crimson and her mouth opened in a roar of pain and indignation. I caught a confused glimpse of Maggie turning away with a dazed, rapt look, her hand again exploring the nakedness of her neck. The long strand of black hair lay tangled now upon the floor.

I started to say something pacifying and explanatory to Otto. But Flora's roars were deafening. Then I was suddenly aware that she was shouting out something; I heard it and knew that the moment of catastrophe had come.

"You fool, you fool! Don't you know who goes to bed with your wife, don't you know who seduces your daughter? Your dear little boy is a devil, devil, devil. Just guess who's in bed all the time with Mummy while you're making a fool of yourself with that slut. Don't you know—"

Flora's voice faded into a choking incoherence of enraged tears. Otto had hold of her arm. He removed her, almost lifting her, to the space at the end of the table. She became still, suddenly terrified.

Otto was very quiet. He looked a little puzzled and stupid, like a large animal which has run into a confined space. He said slowly, "Flora, what are you saying, exactly?"

Flora mumbled, "It's nothing—I was just— Oh!"

Otto must have tightened his grip on her arm. "Flora, repeat what you said just now. At once."

I said, "Otto, please—"

"Shut up. Flora—"

"Oh, don't, don't! I was saying— Oh God, don't

you know— Mummy has a lover. Oh, let me go!"

Otto released her. "But who—?"

"Who do you think? David, of course."

"And you say, you too—?"

"Yes!" Flora cried out, retreating now to the window, rubbing her arm. "Yes, me too! You have been blind, letting it all happen under your nose! Oh, you are stupid!"

Otto stared down at the floor, and I saw his face become red and slowly wrinkle up with anguish like that of a child about to cry. I was desperately sorry for him but much more afraid. I began to edge nearer. As I did so the door quietly opened and David Levkin came in.

Levkin must have realized what had happened as soon as he entered, or more likely he had been listening outside for some time. Flora's cries must have penetrated the whole house. He closed the door and leaned against it, touching it lightly with the palms of his hands. His face had an extraordinary peaceful radiance, like the face of someone quietly meditating some wonderful truth.

Otto said, "Is this true, David, about you and—Isabel—and Flora?"

"Yes, my lord."

I swung the end of the table round out of my way, ready to interpose myself between Otto and David. Flora had mounted onto the window seat. But already Otto had advanced. The big wrinkled, puzzled face stared down, the moist mouth gaping a little. I saw David stiffen, the palms of his hands turning outward in a gesture of donation, his expression radiantly blank. Then with a sort of savage gentleness Otto took him by the shoulders, set him aside, and went slowly out of the door.

I stood in a stupid paralysis of surprise and relief. Then Maggie behind me said something which sounded like a command. I moved quickly after Otto. I passed him in the hall and began to run up the stairs. As I shot past him he began to run too, and we pounded up the stairs together, shaking the house. I reached Isabel's door first, but not soon enough to get through and to bar it against him. I rushed into Isabel's room with Otto close behind me.

Isabel must have known what was happening. She told me afterwards that when she heard the raised voices down below she had composed herself for instant death. She was standing near the window, still in the blue dressing gown, her hand at her throat. She had a forlorn, terrified dignity. I saw her thus for an instant, and in the next moment I was stumbling, holding her up against me, thrusting her into a corner. I really feared that Otto might kill her with a single blow. There was a sound of breaking furniture and cries. Feet thundered across the room. I turned about and realized only a second before the blinding flash and the dreadful pain of it that I was the person that Otto was going to hit.

15 ❧ *Lydia's Sense of Humour*

"Ed, old man, are you all right?"

It was the next day. Black unconsciousness had come upon me with Otto's blow. Black stars expanded into a total night. I came to myself lying on the bed in my own room. Otto must have dragged or carried me there. Otto and Maggie were having some sort of argument about concussion and cracked bones and X-rays which I eventually decided must relate to me. The pain in my face was extreme. It felt as if one side of it had been pushed right into the interior of my head. Attempts to open my eyes brought bright lights and shooting pains and no vision. I groaned and then made out that Maggie and Otto were asking me questions, which I declined to answer. Somewhere a woman was weeping.

The outcome, as I later discovered from Maggie, had been, for all but me, a felicitous one. Otto had stood gazing down at me where I lay sprawled amid the wreckage of Isabel's furniture. Then he had fallen on his knees and seemed to be purged suddenly of his anger. I was got to my own room. Isabel retired behind her locked door. David Levkin had left the house. Maggie and Otto had spent some time tending me and arguing about whether to call a doctor. Eventually I was given some sort of soporific drink and left to fall asleep.

I woke in the morning to more pain and to Otto's large face hovering over me. "Are you all right, Ed?"

"Not specially," I said. "You've probably broken about fifty-seven of those small bones. I shall never be the same again. Oh!" He had put his hand gently on my cheek.

"Maggie thought there was nothing broken. I see you have the good old-fashioned bit of raw beef there. Can you see out of that eye at all?"

"I'd rather not try!"

"Have you forgiven me?"

"Of course, you fool. It was about time somebody hit me anyway."

In an odd way the incident had not only established between Otto and myself a sort of rapport which we had not had since childhood, it had also liberated in us both an extraordinary vitality which was almost like cheerfulness.

"I can't think why I did it!"

I could think of a number of reasons why, but as I had no taste for psychoanalytical discussion I said, "What's the situation this morning?"

"Well, they've gone."

"They?"

"David and Elsa. Gone."

"You mean they've just suddenly cleared off?"

"Well, I cleared them off. I've dismissed them both, sent them away, made an end of it. I was up all night. And not drinking either. At least not much."

I thought: Poor Isabel. But of course it was better so. And poor Otto. "You've broken it all off, Otto?"

"Yes. I realized it was simply an insane situation. Somehow after I'd bashed you I didn't feel angry any more. I just felt what a bloody beastly mess it all was. There was Isabel crying and all the furniture broken and you lying there as if you were dead. For a second I did think I'd killed you. Then Maggie beat me up and I felt rather surprisingly rational after that. Then I knew it really was the moment to make a pretty fierce decision. After this thing about David it was absolutely impossible. I had to get rid of those two. And I had to do it quickly, there was no other way. They were insane-making for all of us. They are fairies, angels, demons. Of course I knew it from the start."

"Angels, demons—yes." I felt a curious sadness.

"So I wrote them a letter saying they must go away at once, and I put in a cheque for David's pay, and Maggie took the letter, and she said they were packing their things anyway. Then I went to bed and I dreamt I was being followed round the house by an enormous black teapot. I tried to telephone for help, but the telephone dial was made of tissue paper—"

"But have they gone?" I ventured to open my other eye but shut it again promptly.

Otto covered his face. His voice shook. "Yes, I think so. I don't want to see them again, I just couldn't trust myself to see either of them. They made me a mad person between them. One has got to put an end to madness somehow."

"And Isabel, have you seen her?"

"No. I'm not sure if I can forgive Isabel. I'm so appallingly connected with her—"

"What about your own misdemeanours?"

"I know. But it doesn't work like that. Maybe we should forgive each other. But it's not so easy. I just feel sick of the whole idea of her at the moment."

"It's just as well you didn't hit her, anyway. How's Flora?"

"Poor little thing. I had a long talk with her last night and she told me everything. God, I should have seen what was happening, I should have looked after her! I was just under a spell."

"Well, you're disenchanted now. Back to real life. I think I'll go home today or tomorrow. Since all the excitements seem to be over." I felt disenchanted myself, as if Otto's blow had knocked all the remains of pretension out of me. I could do nothing for these people. I did not want to witness the pitiful efforts of Otto and Isabel to rebuild their wrecked relationship. I tried to sit up, but my head was heavy with pain and any movement brought twinges of anguish. I struggled feebly while Otto pawed clumsily at the pillows.

"Well," he said, "not quite all the excitements. What do you think of this, which I've just found?" He waved a document in front of my face.

I tried to focus my single eye upon it and began confusedly to read it. Lydia had indeed exercised her sense of humour. *I hereby will and bequeath all of which I die possessed to my beloved and faithful friend, Maria Magistretti.*

16 🦋 *Elsa's Fire Dance*

A solemn family group was assembled in Isabel's room.
The big fire, murmuring, climbing and subsiding with
its own independent life, made the room alternately a
bright and a dim gold, and also uncomfortably hot. It
was still raining outside upon the cold, dripping greenery of an English summer afternoon. The wreckage of
yesterday had been piled in a corner, and the place
seemed less cluttered. Isabel, small, tired, neat in a plain
grey coat and skirt, sat in an armchair. She had been
weeping but was calm now, rather cold. She wore the
detached, rather weary air of an attendant secretary.
Otto, wearing crumpled pyjamas under his sports coat
and trousers, leaned at the mantel. A smell of damp

singeing tweed pervaded the room. It occurred to me that Otto had been weeping too, and I averted my eyes. I wondered if the changelings were indeed gone.

Otto was saying, "Of course there's no reason to suppose she'll want to make any changes at all. After all, she lives here, she's always lived here. She's got nowhere else to go. I fully expect she'll tell us she wants everything to go on as before, and if so of course we should respect her wishes."

I paced by the window, caressing my afflicted eye. The place was hot and very swollen. The eye was almost entirely closed, though effort could produce a watery slit. A bluish-black stain had spread across my brow and down my cheek as far as my mouth. After a disturbed night I felt very tired and rather ill.

"You are deceiving yourself," said Isabel. "That's what would be convenient. But she'll tell us nothing of the sort. She has a will of her own, though she's kept it a secret. She'll break out now, you'll see. She'll make us skip."

It was remarkable how quickly the family had reconstituted itself in the face of a threat to property.

"I do agree with Isabel that she has a will of her own," I said. "But she'll do nothing inconsiderate. I do think it possible she'll insist on ignoring the will."

"After all, it is a bit *odd*," said Otto.

"I see nothing odd about it," said Isabel. "I don't mean she'll turn us out of the house immediately. Oh no, she'll be very reasonable and kind, but she'll treat us as strangers. She hasn't any family sentiment about *us*."

"She must have," I said. "She practically brought us up, Otto and me."

"*She* didn't. I know Otto imagines she pushed his pram, but that's a delusion. She only cared for Lydia. Lydia was good at making people her personal property."

This upset me very much. I certainly now, and with a fresh sharpness, saw Maggie as a separate and private and unpredictable being. I endowed her, as it were, with those human rights, the right of secrecy, the right of surprise. Yet at the same time I could not stop assuming that Maggie—well, that Maggie loved us. It struck me now that it was a rather large assumption and also somewhat unclear. Perhaps I was suffering from a delusion analogous to that of Otto. Our ancestral nurse was, after all, just a sort of legend. Maria Magistretti was quite another matter.

"I can't think why we didn't find the will earlier," Otto was saying. "We looked in that place before."

"Is there much actual *money*, do you think?" I asked.

"Oh, plenty," said Isabel. "Lydia was the meanest of women, but there was lots of money there. And she knew all about the stock market."

"Is the workshop paying its way, Otto?"

"No," he said, avoiding my eye. "It's been—subsidized, in these last years."

"It looks as if I'll have to go out to work!" said Isabel with a nasty laugh.

"How can Lydia have been so bloody tiresome!"

"Well, I've got no reasonable complaint," I said. "Sssh, here she comes."

There was a knock on the door. We all called, "Come in."

A young woman entered, wearing a red dress. The short black hair had been expertly clipped, the serious dark eyes stared from a lean, smooth youthful face. Maggie had acquired what she had never had before, an exterior. She was no longer invisible. And as I stared in amazement at her metamorphosis I recalled suddenly, poignantly, from some much younger age a figure seen in the radiance of my childhood, a dark, slight tutelary goddess.

Otto and I shuffled our feet, making that simulacrum of rising which standing men feel they have to make upon the arrival of an impressive woman, a sort of animal scuffle. Isabel pushed her armchair farther back with a harsh scraping. I cannoned into Otto, trying to place a chair near the fire for Maggie.

She sat down and regarded us.

Otto began, "Maggie, I think you know why we've summoned you." This sounded rather menacing, so he hastily added, "I mean it's all perfectly all right, of course—" This sounded too permissive. He blundered on. "I mean we just felt you might want to tell us—"

"My intentions?"

"Well, yes." Otto, who had been fumbling and trampling during his speech, was clearly now in full retreat. He recoiled almost to the window. His big hands scuffled round the neck of his pyjamas, trying to do up a non-existent button. It had not really occurred to him that Maggie might have intentions. It had not until very lately occurred to me.

"I expect I shall return to Italy later in the year. But I have no immediate plans."

"You'll return to Italy for good?" asked Isabel.

"Oh yes." Maggie answered with a sort of amused casual assurance.

There was an awkward silence. Otto was chewing his knuckles. Isabel was coiled and lowering. I turned to look out at the rain.

"As you may imagine," said Otto at last, "my mother's will came as rather a surprise to us."

"Really."

"What do you intend to do with the house and its contents?" said Isabel.

"Naturally I would give you a first refusal."

"I told you so," said Isabel. She got up and joined me by the window.

"You mean," said Otto slowly, "that you are offering to sell us the house?"

"Well, that would be only proper, wouldn't it?"

Otto thought for a moment. "Yes, I suppose so." He added, "I'm in no position to buy it, unfortunately." Then he said, "Oh God!" and began to laugh in a maniac manner.

Maggie sat and smiled. She crossed her legs and tucked the red dress neatly round her. It was suddenly clear to me that she was acting a part and amusing herself at our expense. She meant nothing of what she said. I said impulsively, "You don't mean this, Maggie. You must come to some sort of civilized arrangement with Otto. Lydia's will was mad and unjust, as you know."

"Not mad. Unjust perhaps. But life is unjust. At least I have always found it so, Edmund."

Her cool words and her use of my name upset me. Surely she, she of all people, could not be unkind? She was where all kindness lived. I stared at her with fascinated doubt, while she regarded us calmly with a sort of diffused gaiety in her face. She seemed like a youthful general confronting some slow, elderly junior officers.

"Oh, don't argue with her!" said Isabel. She went to a chest of drawers and began throwing piles of white nylon underwear out onto the floor.

"What are you doing?" said Otto.

"Packing."

"For God's sake," I said, "what's that noise?"

A strange sound had just become audible far away in the house. We all looked at one another, listening.

There was a dull rumbling which became a sound of running feet and confused voices. I felt a thrill of fear as if it were the onset of some appalling revolution. And for a second it seemed as if it must be connected with Maggie, must be the outcome of the obscure conflict in which we had just been engaged, must be her followers, her people come to take over the house. Isabel gave a cry of alarm. The running feet came nearer. Then the door burst open and Flora came running in. She was drawing someone after her by the hand. It was Elsa.

"Here they are, here they all are!" cried Flora. She thrust Elsa forward.

Maggie had leaped up and moved nearer to me. Isabel retreated, stumbling, into the pile of under-clothes. Otto was bent, covering his face, suddenly shrunk, curled up with pain and shock. Elsa moved to the centre of the room. Her metallic hair fell in long flat strips to her shoulders, like the hair of a statue, and she wore a long shapeless dress which seemed to belong to some other epoch. She looked now as if she were completely mad, the pale wide-nostrilled face twisted and grinning. The wide brow and high cheek-bones shone as if they were oiled. She was both alarming and infinitely pathetic, like something frail and moribund escaped from a hospital.

She seemed to see no one but Otto. She said in a soft whining voice, "No, no, you cannot—come with me now. Come with me. Please, please—" It was like the plaint of an animal.

Otto groaned and then fell heavily forward onto his knees. He spread his hands out in front of him, dropping his head, and grovelled.

"Go away, go away from here." Isabel half stumbled over Otto and then dealt him a savage kick in the side, which tumbled him over onto the floor. She advanced to Elsa and tried to lead her out of the room. Elsa resisted.

Flora had started to utter a high-pitched hysterical "Oh, oh, oh!" Isabel was still gabbling, half angry half frightened, telling Elsa to go. Elsa pushed Isabel violently and then retreated until her feet were almost in the fire. She began to kick the red-hot embers out onto the rug. Isabel screamed. There was a smell of burning, and little tongues of flame spang up at Elsa's capering feet. Otto was sitting on the floor with his hand over his mouth, he seemed unable to move. Elsa was trying to pull a log out of the fire. The heat in the room seemed redoubled, as if we were inside a furnace, and the golden light was everywhere. I cannoned into Isabel, who was retreating, still crying out, as a burning log rolled across the floor. I stamped hard on the smouldering carpet. Flora was shouting, "I hate you, I hate you all." She turned and ran through the door. Maggie called to me, "Go with her, she might—" And I ran out of the room after the girl.

17 ❧ Edmund
in the Enchanted Wood

Flora ran straight down the stairs and out of the house. As I reached the door I saw her receding across the lawn in the wet yellow light. A steady rain was falling. She was making for the stream. I called after her, but the thick oppressive air muffled my voice. I began to run.

The wood was very dark, as if the evening and the night were already installed there, and I ran into a baffle of warm air which seemed full of the beating of birds' wings. The rain inhabited the wood, drumming above and creeping and dripping below. Flora's running steps ahead were heavy yet soft. The race across the lawn had already soaked me, and as I slithered and blundered along the path where I had sauntered so

lately with what now seemed an infinitely younger
Flora, I wondered what I was pursuing. Was I indeed
pursuing or was I fleeing? I called to her again, burst
through a screen of bamboos, and ducked breathlessly
under the first arch of the camellias.

I wanted in that headlong rush to escape from the
brutal chaos of the scene that I had left. It would not,
indeed, be the first time that I had run out of that house
in a sheer horror of what I had seen within. But I ran
too out of some primitive need to catch Flora and
extort from her an absolution which only she could
give: and it was as if in the giving of it she herself
would be somehow replenished and restored. I wanted
to capture her and to retrieve some innocence for us
both, to find in her again the child that I had known.
And I was more rationally afraid that she might indeed, in the hysterical state that she was now in, hurl
herself into the black pool.

A branch of camellia gave me a sharp rap on the
brow just above my bad eye and the pain was so violent for a moment that I had to kneel down on the
ground. The steps receded, echoing a little in the
vaults of the wood. I got up after a moment and went
on more cautiously. The earth was scarcely wet, and
hard and bare as if it had been beaten by the feet of
many dancers. The raindrops clattered on the canopy,
and here and there a pattern of pointed leaves showed
in a dim oval of light. I emerged into the space by the
waterfall.

The dense rain blotted the air, making a dome of yellowish green over the pool. I dashed the water from my eyes. The dark surface was fretted and trembling. The sound of the cascade was merged in the downpour. I could see no one. Then a pale movement caught my eye and I discerned a form halfway up the high bank on the other side of the pool.

Flora had scrambled up the bank, which was steep but not precipitous, toward the high gully down which the stream descended to the fall. Balanced on a rock, one hand grasping a branch above her, she had paused to look back. Her slight dress clung to her figure and she seemed like a naked girl, blurred by the uncertain air, shining and dripping like the rocks about her, a sprite composed of light and water.

I called out to her and she answered something which I could not hear and began climbing again.

I made my way round as far as I could. On one side the rocks fell sheer into the pool, and to reach the place where she was Flora must have passed under the fall. I remembered the slippery ledge of rock behind the plunge of the cascade. The figure of the clambering girl disappeared from view among the precarious saplings above. I dodged into the deafening hollow behind the fall and slithered with squelching shoes in a darkness of spongy moss and ferns. It was very cold. The falling water struck me a violent blow on one shoulder, and I splashed out on the other side.

I could see Flora now directly above me, her legs

straddling a tree, her white skirt spread tight. A long leg dangled, and then she scrambled farther up. A shaft of light, penetrating the rain, cast a haze over the rocks so that the girl seemed to be contained in a golden cylinder. I stood looking up at the floating figure, suddenly dazed by the madness of the pursuit, deafened by the waterfall, frozen and exhausted. I called again. Then it occurred to me that she might be ascending to the road above, where someone could be waiting for her. She might be going to some last unspeakable rendezvous with Levkin. I began to climb.

A stone came flying down with considerable force and just missed my head. Another followed. I flattened myself against the rock. Then something struck me sharply and painfully above the ear. I descended a step or two and received a missile full in the chest. Protecting my face, I slithered back to the platform beside the fall. Quite clearly now above me I could hear Flora's voice crying out, "Rhino! Rhino!" I dodged another stone. Then I glimpsed her through the glittering foliage as with a final kick she reached the level path at the top of the gully. It seemed fruitless to pursue her now. The stones had defeated me. And somehow with that cry of "Rhino!" I grasped her as safe and free and myself as utterly unnecessary. There was nothing I could do for her and nothing she would do for me.

As I turned about I saw across the pool, upon the path which I had just left, the figure of another girl.

The rain was stopping and the sunny hazy light was increasing. The rain abated as I watched, like a curtain drawn steadily back, and the black pool composed the reflection of Maggie. I plunged into the cavern of the fall and received the force of the water upon my other shoulder.

I felt a sudden blank relief at the sight of Maggie, and at the same time became conscious of such an extremity of exhaustion that I could almost have fallen on my hands and knees. I was soaked and shivering, with a most violent pain in my head. I felt sick and giddy. I was about to sit down at the side of the pool, but Maggie had already started to walk back and had entered the wood. Staggering a little, I followed her.

The branches dripped with a hollow sound. "I couldn't catch her. Do you think she'll be all right?"

"Yes, I think so now. I was afraid about the pool."

"So was I. But I think it was just that she couldn't stand it in there. How are things now?"

"I don't know, I couldn't stand it either. I came straight after you."

Maggie moved on just ahead of me, seeming to float over the dark bare ground. I could see her white shoes, scarcely splashed, flicker in the woody twilight. It must be near evening. It had been a long day. We left the camellias and came to the overgrown path beside the stream. Brambles and heavy soaking grass so encumbered my legs that I could scarcely make headway and almost fell down with weariness and exasperation.

The pain in my head was blinding and I was chattering with cold.

"I've lost my shoes." Maggie, who had just tripped over a concealed log, was standing helplessly beside the path, her stockinged feet black with mud.

It was dark in the undergrowth. We beat around ineffectually, poking and pulling and being ferociously torn by brambles and wild roses. Lights seemed to flash every time I bent down, and I saw my questing bloodstained hand as if it belonged to someone else. There was absolutely no sign of Maggie's shoes. They must have become lodged in some thick grassy chamber or fallen into some creature's hole in the river bank. After much scrabbling and scuffling we straightened up and faced each other in the half-dark under tall birch trees. I reeled with tiredness and sickness.

But it was impossible to let her walk barefoot in that thorny jungle. "I suppose, if you don't mind, I'll have to carry you." It sounded ungracious enough.

She said in a subdued way, "Yes, I suppose so," and we faced each other so in a staring awkwardness.

At the moment of picking her up I felt real doubt about whether I could support her at all. I had scarcely, the moment before, been able to drag myself along. To have to carry her on through that weedy, dripping thicket seemed almost too hard, a final idiotic trial, a stupid, blundering end to the madness of the day. I felt I should simply stagger forward and fall with her into the thick briar bush.

I stooped a little towards her and lifted her clear of the ground. She gave a little pressure upon my neck and seemed to fly upwards. She smelled of the rain.

It was not really so difficult to carry her. She was almost miraculously light. The pain seemed gone from my head, and my knees pressed sturdily forward through the yielding green. It was lighter overhead. A great warmth seemed to be flowing from her body into mine. And in a moment or two I was conscious of nothing but the pressure of her slight body against my chest, the firmness of her arm about my neck, and the warm place where my hand passed under her knees. We came out into the open just before reaching the lawn.

I rather slowly set her down. There was something or other I wanted to say. I began, "Maggie—"

She interrupted me with a word which I scarcely heard. I only much later realized what the word was that she had uttered. For at that moment we both saw that a great tongue of yellow flame was issuing from the window of Isabel's room. The house was on fire.

THREE

18 🌹 *Elsa's Rings*

"Is he still in there?"

"Yes."

Otto opened another bottle of champagne. We had been for some very long time shut in that little white hospital waiting room. The cork struck the ceiling and joined other corks on the floor. Otto hit the rim of the glass unsteadily with the neck of the bottle. The white smoky foam rolled over his bandaged hand. He drank hastily and then began to pace again, turning and returning in the confined space. There was a mark upon the wall where he brushed it each time with the swing of his shoulder. Elsa was dead.

"Her dress burned so fast," said Otto. "I grabbed her at once of course and tried to put it out. But she was like a burning torch." He had said this to me ten times, twenty times.

"If only I had not gone away . . ." I had said this to him ten times, twenty times.

"She whirled like a dervish in that room. It would have made no difference."

Who knows? Why had Flora, at that moment of all moments, lured me away like a demoness? If I had behaved differently to Flora, perhaps Elsa would not be dead. I felt that I had killed her, that we had all killed her, and I knew that Otto felt the same.

"She can't have suffered much, can she? Not after the first moment. Surely she can't have suffered. She hardly knew." This also he had said.

"She hardly knew. She was unconscious when I got back. She wasn't conscious again. The doctor said . . ." We were intoning the same things again and again.

"Yet it took so long," said Otto. He spoke in a soft whine of misery quite unlike his usual voice. "She might have known. When they thought she was unconscious, she might have been thinking. She might have been thinking of me, how I'd treated her—"

"Stop it, Otto. And do stop drinking." Otto had been drinking the champagne continuously. He had been grotesquely theoretical in his insistence that it was the only drink one could go on and on with. I could scarcely bear the sight of the bottles.

"It's incredible to me now that I could have done

it," he said, "abandon her like that. I should have managed somehow. I should simply have loved her and
found a way to go on loving her." Her death had made
his love perfect. He saw now only the infinite require-
ment that one person can make upon another. He saw
now that he could have attempted far more perfectly
to meet all his obligations. And with the fearful
strength which her death had given him, it seemed to
him now that he could have succeeded.

I sat on the table. We were like two men in a prison.
There was that sense of there being no more possibili-
ties, of there being only the here and the now and the
this. We had inhabited the little room during the long
terrible time of her unconsciousness. Now it was the
hour of departure but we could not depart. I could see
that Otto could no longer conceive of himself. I
dreaded the task of taking him away.

"Are you sure he's still in there?"

"Yes. I'd have seen him through the glass door. Do
you want to talk to him?"

"No," said Otto. His face still wore the grimace
which I had seen upon it when I ran back from the
wood. The mask had only loosened a little. He passed
me, lumbering to the wall. "You see him, Ed. Find out
what he wants done with—oh God."

We had all been removed to some other plane of
being. Otto was living in torment now what seemed to
him, what perhaps was, the reality of his relation with
Elsa. Something extreme, some truth too appalling to

contemplate and yet arrestingly evident had thrust itself through the surface of our lives like a monstrous hump. And one result of this was that we were all isolated from one another, as if we had been shut into separate cells. Since the catastrophe Otto and David had treated each other with a gentleness, a tenderness almost, which in the midst of such extreme grief on both sides seemed a miracle of attention. There was a respect which resembled love, but no communication. We had each our own Elsa. With a devoted deference Otto had acknowledged David's rights, rights which had seemed pathetically, dreadfully, like property rights, to be the first with Elsa. There had been the arrangements, the vigil, and now—

"I'll speak to him, then," I said. "Shall I ask him to come back—home?" It sounded odd.

"Yes," said Otto. "But he won't come." He lifted his head, and for a moment the mask of pain was curiously cleared and a new Otto looked out, blank, resigned, dispossessed.

"We must look after him."

Otto shook his head. "We can't. *We* can't." The old grimace returned. He said, "Will we ever be the same again, Ed?"

I knew what he meant. It was not just what we had seen and heard in those moments: the blazing room, the screaming women, the handling of that seared flesh. We had seen too much suddenly, too much about mortality and chance, too much about the consequences of our actions, too much about the real nature of the world. I answered, "Yes, unfortunately."

A figure passed quickly behind the glass panel of the door, and I started up. "You'll be all right, Otto? I'll be back directly."

"Yes, go, go."

David had already disappeared. I ran along a white corridor and down some stone steps by a lift shaft. I could hear running feet ahead of me. I began to run too.

I emerged in a long hallway with a vista toward a distant arch. The boy was far ahead, running like a deer. He turned toward the main entrance and was gone. I ran faster down the empty, clean white hall. I passed between pillars and emerged into a busy street, a rainy summer evening. He was already crossing the road. I saw that he had a suitcase.

After so much solitude, so much prison life, I was confused by such a close crowding of faces. A little mild rain was falling. It touched my brow and my hair with a gentle incredulous touch. A yellow sunny light showed buildings vivid and near against a leaden sky. I pursued David across the road.

He was running again. Although he did not look back, he seemed like a man pursued. I was checked by traffic at a side road, and he receded. I could just see his head, distant among many others, and the idea that he might now simply disappear and never be heard of any more filled me with a sudden anguish. I dodged across in front of a lorry and began to run along the edge of the sidewalk, springing into the road in the face of the slow, swarming homecoming crowd.

"David!"

I had almost caught him up when he turned abruptly into a red brick courtyard and I saw we were at the railway station. There were fewer people now. I sprinted and caught his arm.

"Oh, it's you. I thought it was Otto." For a second he looked disappointed. Then he turned and we walked more slowly together into the hall of the station.

"You shouldn't have run like that. You're not going away?"

"Yes." He consulted a timetable on the wall. Then he went to the ticket *guichet*. I stood helplessly, almost shyly, behind him. He too had a new face.

He turned to me more gently now and seemed to expect me to accompany him. "Platform three. Twenty minutes to wait."

We walked over the bridge in silence. He had wept so much that his whole profile was altered, his cheeks and nose shining and swollen. The mask of his expression was different too. The lines of the face were dislocated and incoherent as if the inner spring were broken which had used to wreathe his narrowed eyes with beaming wrinkles. He did not look older, but like a miserable child. My heart was sore for him. But I felt, like Otto, his privileged separateness.

"David, I don't want to trouble you now, but I must. Otto wanted to know—what you want done. Or have you already arranged something?"

"No. Please let Otto arrange it. Forgive me for leaving it to you. You understand, I could not—"

"Yes, yes. That's all right. Have you any special wishes? A Jewish burial?"

"Yes." He seemed a little startled. "Of course. If you will find the leader of the Jewish community he will arrange all, all." He looked already confused and far away. I saw that the tears were coming again and I looked down. I could not bear the mystery of his pain.

I said, "Will you be all right? We wanted you to come home."

He put his suitcase down and put his two hands to his face as if to cool it. His fingers caressed the swollen disfigured cheeks.

"Kind. But I must go. I shall be well."

"Don't grieve," I said idiotically. I felt near to tears myself.

He sighed very deeply. "I knew she was a doomed child. I knew I should have to leave her behind."

The solemnity of the words made me apprehend him as a child himself. "Where are you going, David? Are you going back south to your people? Do not be alone."

"South?" He looked confused for a moment. "No, no. I am going home. To the true north." He smiled a strained smile and rubbed his eyes.

His words puzzled me. "Where?"

"I am going back to Leningrad."

"*Back?*" I stared at him. "But I thought—"

"You thought I was born in Golders Green and that my father was, I forget what, a fur merchant? No. Those were lies. We came from Leningrad like she said, just like she said."

"You mean everything, the whole story?"

"The forest at night, and the searchlights, and my father's hand—all true, every word true just like she said."

I stared at his hot, streaked face. "But why—?"

"Why did I lie? Well, why should I tell the truth, *such* a truth, to anyone who asks? Why should I wear such a story always round my neck and be such a figure to the world? And, oh, there were worse things, worse than she said. I did not want to be a tragic man, to be the suffering one. I wanted to be light, to be new, to be free. . . ." He spoke impatiently, gesturing with his hands as if he were catching the dark fancies that flocked about him.

It was impossible to doubt him now. And as it came to me that he had indeed not escaped his destiny of suffering, the significance of his earlier words came home to me. "Leningrad? But, David, reflect—"

"I want to see the Neva again," he said. "I want to touch those blocks of granite along the quays, to see the Admiralty spire in the sun—"

"David, don't be a perfect fool. You can't go back

there. You might be put in prison. Anything might happen to you."

He spread his hands in a way which made me see that he was Jewish indeed. "Who knows? I believe I would be well, I believe I would be let be. Why should they not let me be? And I am prepared to run the risk of things being otherwise. And even if it were otherwise? It is my own place, and one must suffer in one's own place."

"You are an idiotic little fool," I said. I wanted to impress him, to shake him out of this moment of fantasy. "You are in a completely insane state of mind, an extreme state of mind, at the moment. You want to die too. You simply must not make an irrevocable decision now. You must wait."

He shook his head. "Now is the time, exactly the time, to decide. Do you not realize that we know the truth about ourselves *now?* A truth that will fade."

It was what I had just said myself in answer to Otto's question. It will fade. But I answered him, "Please don't go."

"It is the only place where I am real. They speak the language of my heart."

"They may break your heart. Don't be romantic about it."

"I am in the truth now. And this is a moment for following the truth into whatever folly."

"It will be a very long folly, David."

"Well, so. But I am useless here. You may not understand, but nothing *means* anything to me outside Russia. Your language is dry, dry in my mouth. Here I am a non-man. I should become here a clown, a nothing, some man's toy, as I might have been your brother's toy if he had wished it. I would rather die than be a meaningless man."

"Don't be a lunatic. You may feel this. But think about freedom. You said you wanted to be free, to be light, to be new. Freedom is that one necessary thing. And there, whatever else you have, you will not have that." I looked at my watch. I had ten minutes in which to raise the whole theory of the matter, ten minutes in which to persuade him.

He gave a kind of smile, pushing his full mouth against the misery of his face. "There is no arguing with the bottom of one's heart. Not everyone can have that thing, freedom, and not be ruined by it. It is only one way of life—"

"Idiot! Reflect, reflect! What will you *do* in Leningrad? Imagine, imagine! What about your painting? You spoke to me of that—"

"I burnt those paintings. I am glad you did not see them. I have no talent. And there are things more important."

"That could be so. But for *you*? The question is not what life is best but what life can *you* best live. You *must* consider your own needs, and not just for your own sake either." How to explain *that* to him in ten minutes?

"I have no such needs. Only the ones I spoke of. To be back there. The poet says, 'Russia shines in my heart.' I did not want to leave. One cannot escape from the suffering of the world."

"One need not court it. You remember what you said to me about there being two kinds of Jew—"

"I never really believed it, not for myself. I knew that I would be caught in the end, through her—"

"Have you any family out there?"

"A sister."

"Ah, another sister. What does she do?"

He smiled the painful dragging smile again. "She is a successful person, an engineer."

"I see. Perhaps she has escaped her Jewish destiny."

"Perhaps I am her Jewish destiny."

"You are leaping into the fire."

"It is in our family to do so."

The grimness of the wit shocked me with a terrible sense of his earnestness. I saw him there full of the despair of the very young, the beautiful absoluteness which can drive on toward a lifelong shipwreck. "Do not go, David. Please think for a while anyway. Wait a month or two without deciding. Let me see you again and talk with you. Come and stay at my house and rest and think these things over. Please let me look after you."

He gave me a full stare from wide-open bloodshot eyes. "And what do you think would be the consequence of that? No, no. It is better to do the wrong thing for the right reasons than the right thing for the wrong reasons. Ah, you don't understand—"

I did, however, understand very well. I could have wrung my hands over the tangled mess of human destiny: those half-grasped intimations of right and wrong that drive us out along twilit roads where there is no return.

I said to him harshly, "You can't afford the fare."

He smiled, this time more freely, and I was reminded of Otto's look when the mask seemed to fall from him. "Yes. I have these."

He groped in his pocket and brought out his closed hand. He turned it and opened the palm. There were four diamond rings.

With a shock of mingled horror and pain I recognized them. "So that part of the story was true too."

"I told you it was all true. My father was a provident man. And she—she would not mind—"

"Your father might. He got those rings to help you to get out, not to return."

He shrugged his shoulders. "He got them for our future."

The train came in. David picked up his bag. With a last frenzy of will I took out my pocket book and wrote my address on a page. I thrust the folded paper into his breast pocket. "That's where I live. Think again. Let me know."

He turned to open a carriage door.

"David, have you any messages—for them?"

He paused. "No. The best I can hope is that I shall soon seem as unreal to them as they will seem to me."

"That is not the best, as you know."

"One cannot always achieve the best, as *you* know."

The folded piece of paper fluttered to the ground between us.

The whistle was blowing. He put his foot on the train. With deliberation he took my shoulder and kissed me on both cheeks. "Good-bye, Lord Edmund."

19 ❧ Boxwood

"I dreamt last night," said Otto, "that there was an enormous bird in the house. I think it was a kite—"

"A vulture," I said wearily.

"What? Well, anyway it was following me through the rooms, trailing its wings after it like a sort of train, and I could hear a sort of heavy dragging rustling sound just behind me all the time. I got to the telephone to call for help, but the dial was made of butterscotch, so I didn't dial, and then this bird—"

"Otto, we must decide about Lydia's tombstone."

We were in the workshop. Otto was sitting on the workbench, in a space he had cleared among the tools, eating his lunch. He had just crammed a fat piece of raw carrot into his mouth. As a handful of parsley followed it closely, shreds of munched carrot fell out onto Otto's bare chest and lodged in the curly mat of hair. I was sitting on a block of black Irish limestone. A black pollen covered the floor round about it. Otto had been working.

He rubbed his big unshaven chin with a sandpapery sound. "Yes. I've been thinking. Let's just put 'Beloved Wife of' and 'Beloved Mother of.' The usual stuff. Don't you think? After all, she *was* our mother and she *was* our father's wife. I don't see why she shouldn't put up with it now."

"I agree. I've been thinking that too. And, Otto—"

"Mmm?"

"You do really agree about accepting Maggie's suggestion? You won't throw a fit about it later on?"

"That I keep the house and we split the rest three ways? No, I've no objection at all. It seems rational, doesn't it? The insurance have come up trumps about the fire damage, thank heavens. Lydia's fire extinguishers did a good job. It's only Isabel's room that's a write-off."

I stared at my brother with a mild surprise. I had expected some gestures, some fuss: but Otto seemed to take Maggie's generosity for granted.

"There's plenty, you know," he said, as my wonderment left a suggestive silence.

"Yes, yes, plenty. Well, Otto—"

"Yes, I know. You're just going. Ah, well. Maggie's going too, you know. She's off. I don't suppose we'll see *her* again. It does seem the end of an epoch, doesn't it?"

"How will you manage, Otto, without—without anyone?"

"So you know Isabel's going too? I was right not to stop her, wasn't I? I would never have suggested it. But we were punishing each other. I feel in a curious way it's all for the best, this part of it. I'll manage so long as I can get to the greengrocer's. And I've just learnt how to bake potatoes. All you do—"

"I know, Otto, I've baked many potatoes. You'll manage."

"And Isabel will manage too. She's wonderful, you know."

"I know."

"You don't think I ought to have fought it, tried to persuade her to stay?"

"No."

"I felt—somehow so tired; it was like dropping something very heavy, letting go, letting her go without hatred, setting her free. It seemed essential now, absolutely proper, and I feel so much better about her. You know how when one acts rightly at last it's suddenly very *easy*?"

"I don't, actually."

"Maybe it's just something to do with being in despair. You remember how I said I wanted to be stripped, denuded? Well, it's come. I've become a vegetable. Now there's no hope or fear of anything. I just live in the present. I don't even want to drink. Do you think I'll go on like this, do you think I've really changed?"

"I don't know, Otto."

He did in fact look different. The big flabby face seemed collapsed, fallen apart, as if the strings of anguish had been cut. A vacant, curiously serene light shone from behind. I had not expected this: I had expected a whole drama of violent grief and guilt. I had expected some sort of breakdown. But since he had returned home Otto had been completely quiet. He was working regularly and hardly drinking at all. He did not avoid speaking of Elsa; he seemed better able to think about her than I was. It was not that he made little of her death or failed to see his own share in that destruction. It was that this contemplation had brought him, as he said, to a kind of extremity of which despair was perhaps not the right name. He was beyond the consolations of guilt. He was beyond even the sober machinery of penitence. He was broken and made simple by a knowledge of mortality. Whether he would remain so I could not be certain. But in a way that would have surprised him very much I almost envied him.

"Go and see Isabel before you go, Ed. She's very fond of you. You might be able to help her. She's at the hotel."

"I know. I'm just going there. Then I'll come back and pack."

"Funny for you to go home, won't it be? Us all altered and you just the same. But then you were always miles ahead of us, above us. Sometimes I thought you had a sort of religious vocation, Ed. If we'd been brought up differently—"

"No. It's you who have the religious vocation. I'm just taking a long time to reach the human level. You're the one that watches."

"What one that watches?"

"Never mind. I must be off."

Otto laid aside the onion he had been eating. He wiped his mouth on the long silky black hair which covered the back of his hand. He dusted shreds of carrot off his chest onto his worn and rather smelly corduroy trousers. Gorilla-like he rose, and I rose too for the parting.

My eye was caught by some change of colour on my left among the tall stones. Flora was standing there, so still that she looked for an instant like a pre-Raphaelite girl, all patience, all regard. But then I saw that it was a new Flora. She too had changed. She was neat, tense, modern, a greyhound. As she came forward I flinched before her.

She put her suitcase down while I shuffled my feet in the black limestone dust. She gave me a brief hard glance and then turned severely to Otto. He shrank back a little, looking at her with gaping, drooping mouth, eagerly yet piteously. "Flora—"

"I'm going to stay here now," she said in a high

voice. "I'm going to look after you." She looked, she sounded, like Lydia. Otto wriggled like a deflating balloon and got back onto his table. He smiled a grateful lunatic smile. I moved away.

"You are leaving, Uncle Edmund?"

"Yes, it looks like it. I think I'm being seen off!" I smiled at them both. I was very glad she had come back.

Otto turned his beam upon me. He smiled at me tenderly, exhaustedly, as someone might smile in the presence of death. I had never seen quite this smile before. Flora gave me the severe prim look of the very young. I blessed them both with a salute. "Good-bye, then."

"Good-bye, Ed. By the way, what happened to those boxwood blocks of Father's that you found? I think I might use them after all."

"They're upstairs. I'll just leave them in my room. I'm glad you want them. They've all healed, you know, they're quite sound and whole again. Good-bye, Flora. I hope you've forgiven me."

"Good-bye." She frowned, taking off her coat slowly. "Is your eye better?"

"Yes, much better. It looks funny still but it feels all right." I reached out a hand and she took it. We did not exactly shake hands. It was more like a chaste embrace.

"Good-bye, Ed. Thanks for all. Gosh, I'm a wreck."

"Human lives mend too, mysteriously."

"Mine's the kind that's better cracked. *Ciao*, Ed."

"*Ciao*, Otto."

I left them together and wiped the butter and onion off my hand with a handkerchief.

20 ❧ Isabel
in a Long Perspective

"You know, I think it was Otto that David really loved."

"Maybe," I said.

"He certainly loved being afraid of Otto—and that's a sort of love, isn't it?"

"Yes. There are many sorts of love, Isabel."

She was gradually denuding the scene. The shabby nakedly brown hotel room emerged from under mountains of feathery downy garments which Isabel folded quickly into fantastically small square packages and stowed into suitcases. It was like a metamorphosis of birds.

"I think he wanted Otto to beat him."

"So he didn't tell you where he was going?" I asked.

"No. His letter just said he was going abroad. I daresay it's America. Oh I don't expect to see him again, Edmund, I really don't." She sighed.

I sighed. I had decided not to tell Isabel about my last talk with David. It was better to keep silent and to let the deep logic of the situation remain entirely hid. Simplicity was better than puzzlement. I sat down upon the bed, from which the sheets had already been removed. Our voices were beginning to echo in the empty room. How we had all been stripped, Otto, Isabel, David—and myself.

"America. Yes. Isabel, are you going to be all right? I mean, if you need money of course Otto—"

"Oh, I have some money of my own, don't worry. You aren't shocked at me, are you, Edmund?"

"Shocked? Dear Isabel, of course not! I'm just worried—"

"Yes, I know. But I thought you might be shocked, you're such a very austere and upright sort of person yourself. I know you've hated seeing me and Otto muddling along. You don't think *this* makes it even worse?"

"Isabel, you make me speechless. How can I judge? I just want you both to be happy, and you obviously weren't before. I suppose it's—inevitable, is it, this parting?"

She turned towards me and I saw how different she looked now. Her little intent round face seemed plumper and more youthful, assembled and harmonious, purged of anxiety. A warm radiance shone through like light through alabaster, and her eyes had something of that strange, almost joyful vacancy that I had seen in Otto's. Only the new Isabel seemed, not fallen apart but more centred, more human, more complete. It was not in her to become scattered and crazy.

She said, "Yes. I suppose I knew a long time ago that I was through with Otto. I was through with him ever since he started hitting me. Violence has a terrible effect and in the end one can only go away from it. But I wouldn't see this. I kept being sorry for him in a bad way."

"A bad way?"

"Yes. It wasn't really compassion, it was just an obsessive sense of connection with him, so that being sorry for him was being sorry for myself."

"Are you sorry for him now?"

"I don't know. I can't think about him now. I'll think later and it will be better then. I'm glad Flora turned up. He'll be all right with Flora. He was all right with Lydia until I came along. Flora will keep him in order."

"Don't you want to see her before you go?"

"No. There are moments for just letting things drop in a blank sort of way. We would only hurt each other if I saw her now. Have an apple, Edmund. I got some Cox's Orange specially for you."

"No thanks." I settled back on the bed and looked at her with puzzlement. She was mysteriously, over-

whelmingly, full of herself. I realized she had been, in
the past, only half present. Now she was filled out into
the complete Isabel. The sun, shining in a luminous
blue sky, sent a long beam through the window and
kindled her bright face and her hair as she bent over
the suitcase. Millions of golden points moved about her
in the sunny haze.

"You seem happy," I said almost accusingly.

"No, just real. I can see. That is why you can see
me."

"Couldn't you see before?"

"No. I was living with a black veil tied round my
head. Look here, look out of the window."

I went to her and together we looked out at a yard
of black coal-like earth with a few patches of very
green weeds. Two cars were parked. A tabby cat
emerged from under one of the cars and lounged to
rub itself against a corner of red brick.

"Can you see that cat?"

"Yes, of course."

"Well, until lately I couldn't have seen it at all. Now
it exists, it's there, and while it's there I'm not, I just see
it and let it be. Do you remember that bit in 'The
Ancient Mariner' where he sees the water snakes? 'O
happy living things, no tongue their beauty might
declare!' That's what it's like, suddenly to be able to
see the world and to love it, to be let out of oneself—"

I understood her. "Yes. I'm glad about the cat. But
where are you going to now, Isabel?"

"Back home to Scotland, to my father. He's very much alive and he always detested Otto, so someone will be pleased. I think I shall resume my maiden name."

"What is your maiden name?"

"Learmont."

"That's a good name. Did you know that it was the family name of the Russian poet Lermontov? His ancestors were Scottish—"

"I know, and he was killed in a duel when he was twenty-eight. You said all that to me, Edmund, in exactly those words when we very first met, before I married Otto. Can't you remember?"

I could not remember. I could not out of the pit of time call up that memory of my exchange with the young, distant Isabel. I looked at her, sad and baffled. "No. Odd I should have said those words before and forgotten them. It makes one feel that human beings are just machines after all."

"I've never felt less like a machine. I recall that occasion very well. I've thought about it quite a lot just lately. Help me with the case, will you?"

I pressed my hands down on the suitcase and my sleeve caressed her bare arm. She smelled of a fragrant cosmetic animal warmth. The case clicked shut. The little brown room was bare now, impersonal, waiting for us to go.

"What will you do up there in Scotland? Will you get a job?"

"Well— Sit down, Edmund, will you, you block all the light when you stand up. How hot it is in here— quite Mediterranean weather. And do tuck your long legs out of the way. I've got something to tell you, actually, something rather wonderful."

"What?"

"I'm pregnant."

She moved into the beam of sunlight and the golden dust seemed to settle on her face and her hair. She smiled at me through a gilded haze. I stared in confused amazement, not yet sure what to feel. "David?"

"Yes, of course. Isn't it splendid?" She laughed with a laugh of sheer joy.

"Oh, Isabel—if you're glad, I'm glad, very glad. Does David know—or Otto?"

"No. I shan't tell anyone but you. This is really my business."

"Are you sure?"

"Yes. Now at last I have a future, I possess a future, it's *here*. I've never really owned my life. I shall be independent, *we* shall be independent, now."

"A child," I said. "How strange. It makes everything seem different. A half-Jewish child."

"A half-Scottish child."

"A half-Russian child. A Lermontov. Oh, Isabel, I'm so glad."

"*My* child. As Flora never was. He will be mine, absolutely mine."

Something worried me here. "Well, he'll need, you know—especially if he's a boy—"

"A man around? Yes, I know. Edmund, you wouldn't think of marrying me, would you? I've always liked you so much. Ever since the Learmont conversation."

"I'm sorry—I can't—really I'm most touched, most grateful, but—well, you see, there's someone else."

"Someone else. You are a rum, mysterious fellow, Edmund. All right, all right, don't blush so, though I must say it makes you look most attractive with the remains of that black eye, a sort of wine-stained effect. And, don't worry about me and for heaven's sake don't start apologizing!"

"I am so sorry, Isabel. But you know I'll always be there if you need me, you and young Lermontov."

"I know. Uncle Edmund—*in loco parentis*. All that."

"All that. Good-bye, darling Isabel."

21 ❧ Rome

The kitchen was empty with a disconcertingly final
sort of emptiness. The clock had stopped. The fire was
out. The dresser was bare. Everything was put away
and the cupboards closed and locked. The hot sun
blazed through the William Morris curtains, which
were half drawn, making them glow like stained glass.
The place was scrubbed, naked, abandoned, like a
room awaiting a new tenant. The emptiness frightened
me. I went softly and quickly through to the stairs.
The sunshine did not penetrate here and the shaft of
the house went up, dark and sullen, still smelling of
fire. I listened to the silence of it.

I ran up the stairs. The landing was littered with
charred remains of furniture out of Isabel's room. I

hesitated. I was a man pursued, with only one place to go. I ran up the second flight of stairs to the attic floor where the Italian girl had always lived. I knocked on a door and entered into the dazzling sun.

My relief at finding her still there was so intense it was like the cutting of a cord in me and I almost stumbled. A closed suitcase lay on top of a well-roped trunk. The little white room with its rose-spotted wallpaper had been stripped and tidied. There only remained upon the wall the big familiar map of Italy that Carlotta had pinned up there very many years ago. I entered slowly.

She was standing by the window, lost in the sunlight. "I'm sorry to rush in. I thought for a moment you'd gone."

She said nothing, but moved a little. The dusty, gauzy beam of light made a barrier between us. I began again incoherently. "I'm sorry—"

"You came to say good-bye? That was kind of you." Her voice was dry, slightly rusty, accentless, a homeless, disturbing voice.

I wanted to see her properly and edged round away from the sun. The beam of light fell across her breast, and above it I saw the pale, bony large-eyed face and the cap of dry glossy black hair. It was an old face, a new face, a boy by Titian, the maid of my childhood.

"Well, yes, I—" I felt like a man under a dreadful judgment in a foreign land. I could only stare and supplicate.

"As you see, I am going too, though not just yet. You are catching the afternoon train? There is not much time." The voice was level, almost cruel, but the eyes seemed to get larger and larger.

"No, I mean I don't know. May I—" I looked desperately about. There was a dish of apples on the window sill. "May I have one of these?"

She handed the dish in silence. I took the apple but could not have eaten it, I would have choked. I fumbled it awkwardly against my waistcoat.

"You are going—home?"

"I am going back to Italy, yes. And you are going home too?"

"Yes."

"I wish you a good journey."

I was silent. I could not look at her now, the sense of the cruelty was too great. In another moment I felt I should be saying, "Well, good-bye," and leaving her alone forever in the sunlight. I felt like the poor machine I had just accused myself of being. Some pattern too strong for me was taking me away, curving away back to the old lonely places. I put the apple in my pocket.

Her cotton dress was blue with some kind of white design upon it, a straight, simple dress. I looked at the bosom, I looked at the hem, I looked at the design, stupefied. "Well, I just wanted—" I looked up at her face. It was vacant and merciless as an executioner's. "Well, I just wanted to see if there was anything—"

"Anything you could do for me? No, thank you."

"Oh stop it, Maggie!"

"Stop what?"

The repetition of the words shot me through with a sort of dry anguish, a sense of my futility. I felt powerless, weightless, paralysed like a man in a dream.

I said, mumbling, "I'm sorry, I'm very stupid. I must be tired. I'll leave you to pack. I suppose I must catch that train." The old pattern took hold of me, it herded me along like a brute. I started to shamble wretchedly toward the door.

I trod awkwardly on something which was out in the middle of the floor. It was a pair of white shoes. Grunting apologies, I stooped to set them upright again, and then rose slowly, holding one of them in my hand. Like a man in a fairy tale who is given an obscure sign, I held onto the shoe with a sudden blind attention, not yet sure what I was being told.

I said slowly, "But these were the shoes you lost in the wood, weren't they? So you found them again after all?"

She darted at me and almost wrenched the shoe out of my hand and tossed it onto the bed. It was like an attack.

"I didn't find them. I never lost them."

The shock of her movement and her sudden proximity took the sense out of her words for a moment. "How do you mean, you never lost them?"

"They were never lost. They were in my pocket.

Now good-bye Edmund. It is time for your train. Good-bye, good-bye—"

I picked up the shoe again. I sat down heavily upon the bed. I said, "I'm not going."

There was a long but utterly different silence. The room moved like a kaleidoscope and settled down again, larger, enclosed, safe. I said, "Maria."

That was the word which the Italian girl had uttered as we came out of the wood together on that day which now seemed so long ago. It was a charm which had been given me for a later use. My tongue was freed to use it now.

She came and sat at the other end of the bed and we gazed at each other. I could not remember that I had looked at anyone in quite that way before: when one is all vision and the other face enters into one's own. I was aware too of a bodily feeling which was not exactly desire but was rather something to do with time, a sense of the present being infinitely large.

She did not smile, but the severe mask was changed, softened into a sort of rueful, relieved exhaustion. She looked suddenly relaxed and very tired, like someone who has travelled a long way and arrived.

She said, "I was not very clever with you, was I."

Her words stirred me and touched me so poignantly that I could have moaned over them. But I said calmly, "You were certainly very harsh with me just now. Would you really have let me go away?"

She looked at me intently for a moment and then shook her head.

I hid my face against the shoe. Gratitude came as a physical pain, and then I too felt a relaxed tiredness which was a pure joy.

She went on, "I found I couldn't talk to you and yet I knew that once I started it would be quite easy. Yet I couldn't stop being awkward and hostile and making you awkward too." She spoke it with an air of simple explanation.

I said in the same tone, "I know. I think I was very stupid. But I would not have gone away."

"You might have done. You may yet. I just wanted us to be present to each other for a moment."

"We are certainly that." I felt a calm, blissful sense of power which was at the same time a frenzy of humility. I was released and armed. Now I could act humanly, think, wish, reflect, speak. I gripped the shoe in my hand. I wanted to kneel on the floor. But I said coolly, "Why did you decide to let us see the will?"

"I had to make you notice me somehow!"

I bowed my head. "I am a crude object!" It was true. The money had certainly attracted my attention. But of course I had known all along. Or had I?

"Then I nearly gave up because of her."

"Lydia?"

"Elsa."

The two names composed a shadowy presence, as if

we had looked up to find ourselves close to some great tower. I said, "You mean when Elsa died it took away all purposes."

"Yes. But perhaps in the end it simply changed us into ourselves. We all died for a moment, but then what came after had a greater certainty."

It seemed odd to me that she should speak of dying with Elsa. We were indeed, like all human beings, brief mourners. But what about Lydia? I was about to speak of her, but checked myself. That would come later, much later. How was I so sure that there was so much future? I said, "I think Otto has died for more than a moment."

I recalled Otto's crazy destroyed face. And then I suddenly apprehended myself at a parting of the ways. It was not yet too late. Flora had called my life a crippled life. Was that the truth of it? Ought I not now to jump up and run from the room before I should have meddled decisively, catastrophically, with myself? Some great force was poised, not yet released. This obscure, allusive conversation could be terminated as abruptly as it had started. I could still go away down the stairs and out of the house. Ought I not to return to my solitude and my simplicities and study once more to gain by patience what had come, perhaps, to Otto in a moment of flame? Otto and I had in some sense changed places, passing each other on the way, and now it was I who had the fool's part. What was the value, what had been the value, of my long meditation? I had had no power here to heal the ills of others, I had merely discovered my own. I had thought to have passed beyond life, but now it seemed to me that I had simply evaded it. I had not passed beyond anything; I was a false religious, a frightened man.

It was only for a second that I saw her as a temptress. At the next moment her face was the face of happiness, something which I had scarcely ever seen and which I had long ago stopped seeking. And even as I apprehended her as my happiness I apprehended her too as my unhappiness. I recalled David's words, that one must suffer in one's own place. Whatever joy or sorrow might come to me from this would be real and my own, I would be living at my own level and suffering in my own place. There was only one person in the world for whom I could be complete, and I had found her. And with that of course I thought of Lydia and of Lydia's mystery, which I was now in some sense inheriting, and I knew that at some time in the future the Italian girl would speak to me Lydia's true epitaph.

I rubbed my eyes. I did not want to have, yet, so many thoughts. I wanted to be, for a while, perhaps for the first time, diminished and simple, and to deal simply for better or worse with another person. I saw her now, a girl, a stranger, and yet the most familiar person in the world: my Italian girl, and yet also the first woman, as strange as Eve to the dazed awakening of Adam. She was there, separately and authoritatively there, like the cat which Isabel had shown me from the window. The fleeing woman fled no longer; she had turned about.

I said, "It's odd, I scarcely know you. Yet I feel now for the first time that my past is really continuous with my future. Were you really there *then*, was it really you?"

She smiled at last and patted back the short hair to which she had not yet got accustomed. "You were so very beautiful, Edmund, when you were seventeen."

I gave a sort of groan. "But now, what am I now?" I scarcely knew what I looked like any more. I had had no images of myself. That too I would have to learn.

"*Si vedra. Non aver paura.*"

The Italian words were like a transforming bell. I felt suddenly the heat of the room, the sweet presence of the sun: to live in the sun, to love in the open. I said, "You are going to Italy?"

"Yes—to Rome."

I took a deep breath. I was suddenly trembling violently. "May I drive you there in my car?"

Her answer was a nod, a sigh. At the same time she put her finger to her lips.

I understood. I looked at her hands. They were still as distant as stars. I drew back. There was a time ahead.

I took the apple from my pocket and began to eat it. I said, "I'll go and pack. Then we can think about times and places. Why, it's Italian weather already."

As I went to the door I paused beside the map of Italy. The route, yes, that too we would have to discuss. I drew my finger along the Via Aurelia. Genova, Pisa, Livorno, Grosseto, Civitavecchia, Roma.